The Poor Clare
&
The Doom of the Griffiths

Elizabeth Cleghorn Gaskell

The Poor Clare & The Doom of the Griffiths

Copyright © 2021 Bibliotech Press

The present edition is a reproduction of previous publication of this classic work. Minor typographical errors may have been corrected without note; however, for an authentic reading experience the spelling, punctuation, and capitalization have been retained from the original text.

ISBN: 978-1-63637-463-5

CONTENTS

THE POOR CLARE

CHAPTER I

December 12th, 1747.—My life has been strangely bound up with extraordinary incidents, some of which occurred before I had any connection with the principal actors in them, or indeed, before I even knew of their existence. I suppose, most old men are, like me, more given to looking back upon their own career with a kind of fond interest and affectionate remembrance, than to watching the events—though these may have far more interest for the multitude—immediately passing before their eyes. If this should be the case with the generality of old people, how much more so with me! . . . If I am to enter upon that strange story connected with poor Lucy, I must begin a long way back. I myself only came to the knowledge of her family history after I knew her; but, to make the tale clear to any one else, I must arrange events in the order in which they occurred—not that in which I became acquainted with them.

There is a great old hall in the north-east of Lancashire, in a part they called the Trough of Bolland, adjoining that other district named Craven. Starkey Manor-house is rather like a number of rooms clustered round a gray, massive, old keep than a regularly-built hall. Indeed, I suppose that the house only consisted of a great tower in the centre, in the days when the Scots made their raids terrible as far south as this; and that after the Stuarts came in, and there was a little more security of property in those parts, the Starkeys of that time added the lower building, which runs, two stories high, all round the base of the keep. There has been a grand garden laid out in my days, on the southern slope near the house; but when I first knew the place, the kitchen-garden at the farm was the only piece of cultivated ground belonging to it. The deer used to come within sight of the drawing-room windows, and might have browsed quite close up to the house if they had not been too wild and shy. Starkey Manor-house itself stood on a projection or peninsula of high land, jutting out from the abrupt hills that form the sides of the Trough of Bolland. These hills were rocky and bleak enough towards their summit; lower down they were clothed with tangled copsewood and green depths of fern, out of which a gray giant of an ancient forest-tree would tower here and there, throwing up its ghastly white branches, as if in imprecation, to the sky. These trees, they told me, were the remnants of that forest which existed in the days of the Heptarchy, and were even then noted as landmarks. No wonder that their upper and more exposed branches were leafless, and that the dead bark had peeled away, from sapless old age.

Not far from the house there were a few cottages, apparently, of the same date as the keep; probably built for some retainers of the family, who sought shelter—they and their families and their small flocks and herds—at the hands of their feudal lord. Some of them had pretty much fallen to decay. They were built in a strange fashion. Strong beams had been sunk firm in the ground

2

at the requisite distance, and their other ends had been fastened together, two and two, so as to form the shape of one of those rounded waggon-headed gipsy-tents, only very much larger. The spaces between were filled with mud, stones, osiers, rubbish, mortar—anything to keep out the weather. The fires were made in the centre of these rude dwellings, a hole in the roof forming the only chimney. No Highland hut or Irish cabin could be of rougher construction.

The owner of this property, at the beginning of the present century, was a Mr. Patrick Byrne Starkey. His family had kept to the old faith, and were stanch Roman Catholics, esteeming it even a sin to marry any one of Protestant descent, however willing he or she might have been to embrace the Romish religion. Mr. Patrick Starkey's father had been a follower of James the Second; and, during the disastrous Irish campaign of that monarch he had fallen in love with an Irish beauty, a Miss Byrne, as zealous for her religion and for the Stuarts as himself. He had returned to Ireland after his escape to France, and married her, bearing her back to the court at St. Germains. But some licence on the part of the disorderly gentlemen who surrounded King James in his exile, had insulted his beautiful wife, and disgusted him; so he removed from St. Germains to Antwerp, whence, in a few years' time, he quietly returned to Starkey Manor-house—some of his Lancashire neighbours having lent their good offices to reconcile him to the powers that were. He was as firm a Catholic as ever, and as stanch an advocate for the Stuarts and the divine rights of kings; but his religion almost amounted to asceticism, and the conduct of these with whom he had been brought in such close contact at St.

3

Germains would little bear the inspection of a stern moralist. So he gave his allegiance where he could not give his esteem, and learned to respect sincerely the upright and moral character of one whom he yet regarded as an usurper. King William's government had little need to fear such a one. So he returned, as I have said, with a sobered heart and impoverished fortunes, to his ancestral house, which had fallen sadly to ruin while the owner had been a courtier, a soldier, and an exile. The roads into the Trough of Bolland were little more than cart-ruts; indeed, the way up to the house lay along a ploughed field before you came to the deer-park. Madam, as the country-folk used to call Mrs. Starkey, rode on a pillion behind her husband, holding on to him with a light hand by his leather riding-belt. Little master (he that was afterwards Squire Patrick Byrne Starkey) was held on to his pony by a serving-man. A woman past middle age walked, with a firm and strong step, by the cart that held much of the baggage; and high up on the mails and boxes, sat a girl of dazzling beauty, perched lightly on the topmost trunk, and swaying herself fearlessly to and fro, as the cart rocked and shook in the heavy roads of late autumn. The girl wore the Antwerp faille, or black Spanish mantle over her head, and altogether her appearance was such that the old cottager, who described the possession to me many years after, said that all the country-folk took her for a foreigner. Some dogs, and the boy who held them in charge, made up the company. They rode silently along, looking with grave, serious eyes at the people, who came out of the scattered cottages to bow or curtsy to the real Squire, "come back at last," and gazed after the little procession with gaping wonder, not deadened by the sound of the foreign language in which the few necessary words

4

that passed among them were spoken. One lad, called from his staring by the Squire to come and help about the cart, accompanied them to the Manor-house. He said that when the lady had descended from her pillion, the middle-aged woman whom I have described as walking while the others rode, stepped quickly forward, and taking Madam Starkey (who was of a slight and delicate figure) in her arms, she lifted her over the threshold, and set her down in her husband's house, at the same time uttering a passionate and outlandish blessing. The Squire stood by, smiling gravely at first; but when the words of blessing were pronounced, he took off his fine feathered hat, and bent his head. The girl with the black mantle stepped onward into the shadow of the dark hall, and kissed the lady's hand; and that was all the lad could tell to the group that gathered round him on his return, eager to hear everything, and to know how much the Squire had given him for his services.

From all I could gather, the Manor-house, at the time of the Squire's return, was in the most dilapidated state. The stout gray walls remained firm and entire; but the inner chambers had been used for all kinds of purposes. The great withdrawing-room had been a barn; the state tapestry-chamber had held wool, and so on. But, by-and-by, they were cleared out; and if the Squire had no money to spend on new furniture, he and his wife had the knack of making the best of the old. He was no despicable joiner; she had a kind of grace in whatever she did, and imparted an air of elegant picturesqueness to whatever she touched. Besides, they had brought many rare things from the Continent; perhaps I should rather say, things that were rare in that part of England—carvings, and crosses, and beautiful

5

pictures. And then, again, wood was plentiful in the Trough of Bolland, and great log-fires danced and glittered in all the dark, old rooms, and gave a look of home and comfort to everything.

Why do I tell you all this? I have little to do with the Squire and Madame Starkey; and yet I dwell upon them, as if I were unwilling to come to the real people with whom my life was so strangely mixed up. Madam had been nursed in Ireland by the very woman who lifted her in her arms, and welcomed her to her husband's home in Lancashire. Excepting for the short period of her own married life, Bridget Fitzgerald had never left her nursling. Her marriage—to one above her in rank—had been unhappy. Her husband had died, and left her in even greater poverty than that in which she was when he had first met with her. She had one child, the beautiful daughter who came riding on the waggon-load of furniture that was brought to the Manor-house. Madame Starkey had taken her again into her service when she became a widow. She and her daughter had followed "the mistress" in all her fortunes; they had lived at St. Germains and at Antwerp, and were now come to her home in Lancashire. As soon as Bridget had arrived there, the Squire gave her a cottage of her own, and took more pains in furnishing it for her than he did in anything else out of his own house. It was only nominally her residence. She was constantly up at the great house; indeed, it was but a short cut across the woods from her own home to the home of her nursling. Her daughter Mary, in like manner, moved from one house to the other at her own will. Madam loved both mother and child dearly. They had great influence over her, and, through her, over her husband. Whatever Bridget or Mary willed was sure to come to pass.

6

They were not disliked; for, though wild and passionate, they were also generous by nature. But the other servants were afraid of them, as being in secret the ruling spirits of the household. The Squire had lost his interest in all secular things; Madam was gentle, affectionate, and yielding. Both husband and wife were tenderly attached to each other and to their boy; but they grew more and more to shun the trouble of decision on any point; and hence it was that Bridget could exert such despotic power. But if everyone else yielded to her "magic of a superior mind," her daughter not unfrequently rebelled. She and her mother were too much alike to agree. There were wild quarrels between them, and wilder reconciliations. There were times when, in the heat of passion, they could have stabbed each other. At all other times they both—Bridget especially—would have willingly laid down their lives for one another. Bridget's love for her child lay very deep—deeper than that daughter ever knew; or I should think she would never have wearied of home as she did, and prayed her mistress to obtain for her some situation—as waiting maid—beyond the seas, in that more cheerful continental life, among the scenes of which so many of her happiest years had been spent. She thought, as youth thinks, that life would last for ever, and that two or three years were but a small portion of it to pass away from her mother, whose only child she was. Bridget thought differently, but was too proud ever to show what she felt. If her child wished to leave her, why—she should go. But people said Bridget became ten years older in the course of two months at this time. She took it that Mary wanted to leave her. The truth was, that Mary wanted for a time to leave the place, and to seek some change, and would thankfully have taken her mother with her. Indeed when Madam Starkey had gotten her a situation with some grand lady abroad, and the time drew near for her to go, it was Mary who clung to her mother with passionate embrace, and, with floods of tears, declared that she would never leave her; and it was Bridget, who at last loosened her arms, and, grave and tearless herself, bade her keep her word, and go forth into the wide world. Sobbing aloud, and looking back continually, Mary went away. Bridget was still as death, scarcely drawing her breath, or closing her stony eyes; till at last she turned back into her cottage, and heaved a ponderous old settle against the door. There she sat, motionless, over the gray ashes of her extinguished fire, deaf to Madam's sweet voice, as she begged leave to enter and comfort her nurse. Deaf, stony, and motionless, she sat for more than twenty hours; till, for the third time, Madam came across the snowy path from the great house, carrying with her a young spaniel, which had been Mary's pet up at the hall; and which had not ceased all night long to seek for its absent mistress, and to whine and moan after her. With tears Madam told this story, through the closed door—tears excited by the terrible look of anguish, so steady, so immovable—so the same to-day as it was yesterday—on her nurse's face. The little creature in her arms began to utter its piteous cry, as it shivered with the cold. Bridget stirred; she moved—she listened. Again that long whine; she thought it was for her daughter; and what she had denied to her nursling and mistress she granted to the dumb creature that Mary had cherished. She opened the door, and took the dog from Madam's arms. Then Madam came in, and kissed and comforted the old woman, who took but little notice of her or anything. And sending up Master Patrick to the hall for fire and food, the sweet young lady never left her nurse all that night.

8

Next day, the Squire himself came down, carrying a beautiful foreign picture—Our Lady of the Holy Heart, the Papists call it. It is a picture of the Virgin, her heart pierced with arrows, each arrow representing one of her great woes. That picture hung in Bridget's cottage when I first saw her; I have that picture now.

Years went on. Mary was still abroad. Bridget was still and stern, instead of active and passionate. The little dog, Mignon, was indeed her darling. I have heard that she talked to it continually; although, to most people, she was so silent. The Squire and Madam treated her with the greatest consideration, and well they might; for to them she was as devoted and faithful as ever. Mary wrote pretty often, and seemed satisfied with her life. But at length the letters ceased—I hardly know whether before or after a great and terrible sorrow came upon the house of the Starkeys. The Squire sickened of a putrid fever; and Madam caught it in nursing him, and died. You may be sure, Bridget let no other woman tend her but herself; and in the very arms that had received her at her birth, that sweet young woman laid her head down, and gave up her breath. The Squire recovered, in a fashion. He was never strong—he had never the heart to smile again. He fasted and prayed more than ever; and people did say that he tried to cut off the entail, and leave all the property away to found a monastery abroad, of which he prayed that some day little Squire Patrick might be the reverend father. But he could not do this, for the strictness of the entail and the laws against the Papists. So he could only appoint gentlemen of his own faith as guardians to his son, with many charges about the lad's soul, and a few about the land, and the way it was to be held while he was a minor. Of course, Bridget was not forgotten.

He sent for her as he lay on his death-bed, and asked her if she would rather have a sum down, or have a small annuity settled upon her. She said at once she would have a sum down; for she thought of her daughter, and how she could bequeath the money to her, whereas an annuity would have died with her. So the Squire left her her cottage for life, and a fair sum of money. And then he died, with as ready and willing a heart as, I suppose, ever any gentleman took out of this world with him. The young Squire was carried off by his guardians, and Bridget was left alone.

I have said that she had not heard from Mary for some time. In her last letter, she had told of travelling about with her mistress, who was the English wife of some great foreign officer, and had spoken of her chances of making a good marriage, without naming the gentleman's name, keeping it rather back as a pleasant surprise to her mother; his station and fortune being, as I had afterwards reason to know, far superior to anything she had a right to expect. Then came a long silence; and Madam was dead, and the Squire was dead; and Bridget's heart was gnawed by anxiety, and she knew not whom to ask for news of her child. She could not write, and the Squire had managed her communication with her daughter. She walked off to Hurst; and got a good priest there—one whom she had known at Antwerp—to write for her. But no answer came. It was like crying into the' awful stillness of night.

One day, Bridget was missed by those neighbours who had been accustomed to mark her goings-out and comings-in. She had never been sociable with any of them; but the sight of her had become a part of their daily lives, and slow wonder arose in their minds, as morning after morning came, and her house-door remained closed, her window dead from any glitter, or light of fire within. At length, some one tried the door; it was locked. Two or three laid their heads together, before daring to look in through the blank unshuttered window. But, at last, they summoned up courage; and then saw that Bridget's absence from their little world was not the result of accident or death, but of premeditation. Such small articles of furniture as could be secured from the effects of time and damp by being packed up, were stowed away in boxes. The picture of the Madonna was taken down, and gone. In a word, Bridget had stolen away from her home, and left no trace whither she was departed. I knew afterwards, that she and her little dog had wandered off on the long search for her lost daughter. She was too illiterate to have faith in letters, even had she had the means of writing and sending many. But she had faith in her own strong love, and believed that her passionate instinct would guide her to her child. Besides, foreign travel was no new thing to her, and she could speak enough of French to explain the object of her journey, and had, moreover, the advantage of being, from her faith, a welcome object of charitable hospitality at many a distant convent. But the country people round Starkey Manor-house knew nothing of all this. They wondered what had become of her, in a torpid, lazy fashion, and then left off thinking of her altogether. Several years passed. Both Manor-house and cottage were deserted. The young Squire lived far away under the direction of his guardians. There were inroads of wool and corn into the sitting-rooms of the Hall; and there was some low talk, from time to time, among the hinds and country people whether it would not be as well to break into old Bridget's cottage, and save such of her goods as were left from the moth and rust which must be making sad havoc. But this idea was always quenched by the recollection of her strong character and passionate anger; and tales of her masterful spirit, and vehement force of will, were whispered about, till the very thought of offending her, by touching any article of hers, became invested with a kind of horror: it was believed that, dead or alive, she would not fail to avenge it.

Suddenly she came home; with as little noise or note of preparation as she had departed. One day some one noticed a thin, blue curl of smoke ascending from her chimney. Her door stood open to the noonday sun; and, ere many hours had elapsed, some one had seen an old travel-and-sorrow-stained woman dipping her pitcher in the well; and said, that the dark, solemn eyes that looked up at him were more like Bridget Fitzgerald's than any one else's in this world; and yet, if it were she, she looked as if she had been scorched in the flames of hell, so brown, and scared, and fierce a creature did she seem. By-and-by many saw her; and those who met her eye once cared not to be caught looking at her again. She had got into the habit of perpetually talking to herself; nay, more, answering herself, and varying her tones according to the side she took at the moment. It was no wonder that those who dared to listen outside her door at night believed that she held converse with some spirit; in short, she was unconsciously earning for herself the dreadful reputation of a witch.

Her little dog, which had wandered half over the Continent with her, was her only companion; a dumb remembrancer of happier days. Once he was ill; and she carried him more than three miles, to ask about his management from one who had been groom to the last Squire, and had then been noted for his skill in all diseases of animals. Whatever this man did, the dog recovered; and they who heard her thanks, intermingled with blessings (that were rather promises of good fortune than prayers), looked grave at his good luck when, next year, his ewes twinned, and his meadow-grass was heavy and thick.

Now it so happened that, about the year seventeen hundred and eleven, one of the guardians of the young squire, a certain Sir Philip Tempest, bethought him of the good shooting there must be on his ward's property; and in consequence he brought down four or five gentlemen, of his friends, to stay for a week or two at the Hall. From all accounts, they roystered and spent pretty freely. I never heard any of their names but one, and that was Squire Gisborne's. He was hardly a middle-aged man then; he had been much abroad, and there, I believe, he had known Sir Philip Tempest, and done him some service. He was a daring and dissolute fellow in those days: careless and fearless, and one who would rather be in a quarrel than out of it. He had his fits of ill-temper besides, when he would spare neither man nor beast. Otherwise, those who knew him well, used to say he had a good heart, when he was neither drunk, nor angry, nor in any way vexed. He had altered much when I came to know him.

One day, the gentlemen had all been out shooting, and with but little success, I believe; anyhow, Mr. Gisborne had none, and was in a black humour accordingly. He was coming home, having his gun loaded, sportsman-like, when little Mignon crossed his path, just as he turned out of the wood by Bridget's cottage. Partly for wantonness, partly to vent his spleen upon some living creature. Mr. Gisborne took his gun, and fired—he had better have never fired gun again, than aimed that unlucky shot, he hit Mignon, and at the creature's sudden cry, Bridget came out, and saw at a glance what had been done. She took Mignon up in her arms, and looked hard at the wound; the poor dog looked at her with his glazing eyes, and tried to wag his tail and lick her hand, all covered with blood. Mr. Gisborne spoke in a kind of sullen penitence:

"You should have kept the dog out of my way—a little poaching varmint."

At this very moment, Mignon stretched out his legs, and stiffened in her arms—her lost Mary's dog, who had wandered and sorrowed with her for years. She walked right into Mr. Gisborne's path, and fixed his unwilling, sullen look, with her dark and terrible eye.

"Those never throve that did me harm," said she. "I'm alone in the world, and helpless; the more do the saints in heaven hear my prayers. Hear me, ye blessed ones! hear me while I ask for sorrow on this bad, cruel man. He has killed the only creature that loved me—the dumb beast that I loved. Bring down heavy sorrow on his head for it, O ye saints! He thought that I was helpless, because he saw me lonely and poor; but are not the armies of heaven for the like of me?"

"Come, come," said he, half remorseful, but not one whit afraid. "Here's a crown to buy thee another dog. Take it, and leave off cursing! I care none for thy threats."

"Don't you?" said she, coming a step closer, and changing her

14

imprecatory cry for a whisper which made the gamekeeper's lad, following Mr. Gisborne, creep all over. "You shall live to see the creature you love best, and who alone loves you—ay, a human creature, but as innocent and fond as my poor, dead darling— you shall see this creature, for whom death would be too happy, become a terror and a loathing to all, for this blood's sake. Hear me, O holy saints, who never fail them that have no other help!"

She threw up her right hand, filled with poor Mignon's life- drops; they spirted, one or two of them, on his shooting-dress,— an ominous sight to the follower. But the master only laughed a little, forced, scornful laugh, and went on to the Hall. Before he got there, however, he took out a gold piece, and bade the boy carry it to the old woman on his return to the village. The lad was "afeared," as he told me in after years; he came to the cottage, and hovered about, not daring to enter. He peeped through the window at last; and by the flickering wood-flame, he saw Bridget kneeling before the picture of Our Lady of the Holy Heart, with dead Mignon lying between her and the Madonna. She was praying wildly, as her outstretched arms betokened. The lad shrunk away in redoubled terror; and contented himself with slipping the gold piece under the ill- fitting door. The next day it was thrown out upon the midden; and there it lay, no one daring to touch it.

Meanwhile Mr. Gisborne, half curious, half uneasy, thought to lessen his uncomfortable feelings by asking Sir Philip who Bridget was? He could only describe her—he did not know her name. Sir Philip was equally at a loss. But an old servant of the Starkeys, who had resumed his livery at the Hall on this occasion—a scoundrel whom Bridget had saved from dismissal more than once during her palmy days—said:—

"It will be the old witch, that his worship means. She needs a ducking, if ever a woman did, does that Bridget Fitzgerald."

"Fitzgerald!" said both the gentlemen at once. But Sir Philip was the first to continue:—

"I must have no talk of ducking her, Dickon. Why, she must be the very woman poor Starkey bade me have a care of; but when I came here last she was gone, no one knew where. I'll go and see her to-morrow. But mind you, sirrah, if any harm comes to her, or any more talk of her being a witch—I've a pack of hounds at home, who can follow the scent of a lying knave as well as ever they followed a dog-fox; so take care how you talk about ducking a faithful old servant of your dead master's."

"Had she ever a daughter?" asked Mr. Gisborne, after a while.

"I don't know—yes! I've a notion she had; a kind of waiting woman to Madam Starkey."

"Please your worship," said humbled Dickon, "Mistress Bridget had a daughter—one Mistress Mary—who went abroad, and has never been heard on since; and folk do say that has crazed her mother."

Mr. Gisborne shaded his eyes with his hand.

"I could wish she had not cursed me," he muttered. "She may have power—no one else could." After a while, he said aloud, no one understanding rightly what he meant, "Tush! it is impossible!"—and called for claret; and he and the other gentlemen set-to to a drinking-bout.

CHAPTER II

I now come to the time in which I myself was mixed up with the people that I have been writing about. And to make you understand how I became connected with them, I must give you some little account of myself. My father was the younger son of a Devonshire gentleman of moderate property; my eldest uncle succeeded to the estate of his forefathers, my second became an eminent attorney in London, and my father took orders. Like most poor clergymen, he had a large family; and I have no doubt was glad enough when my London uncle, who was a bachelor, offered to take charge of me, and bring me up to be his successor in business.

In this way I came to live in London, in my uncle's house, not far from Gray's Inn, and to be treated and esteemed as his son, and to labour with him in his office. I was very fond of the old gentleman. He was the confidential agent of many country squires, and had attained to his present position as much by knowledge of human nature as by knowledge of law; though he was learned enough in the latter. He used to say his business was law, his pleasure heraldry. From his intimate acquaintance with family history, and all the tragic courses of life therein involved, to hear him talk, at leisure times, about any coat of arms that came across his path was as good as a play or a romance. Many cases of disputed property, dependent on a love of genealogy, were brought to him, as to a great authority on such points. If the lawyer who came to consult him was young, he would take no fee, only give him a long lecture on the importance of attending to heraldry; if the lawyer was of mature age and good standing, he would mulct him pretty well, and abuse him to me afterwards as negligent of one great branch of the profession. His house was in a stately new street called Ormond Street, and in it he had a handsome library; but all the books treated of things that were past; none of them planned or looked forward into the future. I worked away—partly for the sake of my family at home, partly because my uncle had really taught me to enjoy the kind of practice in which he himself took such delight. I suspect I worked too hard; at any rate, in seventeen hundred and eighteen I was far from well, and my good uncle was disturbed by my ill looks.

One day, he rang the bell twice into the clerk's room at the dingy office in Grey's Inn Lane. It was the summons for me, and I went into his private room just as a gentleman—whom I knew well enough by sight as an Irish lawyer of more reputation than he deserved—was leaving.

My uncle was slowly rubbing his hands together and considering. I was there two or three minutes before he spoke. Then he told me that I must pack up my portmanteau that very afternoon, and start that night by post-horse for West Chester. I should get there, if all went well, at the end of five days' time, and must then wait for a packet to cross over to Dublin; from thence I must proceed to a certain town named Kildoon, and in that neighbourhood I was to remain, making certain inquiries as to the existence of any descendants of the younger branch of a family to whom some valuable estates had descended in the female line. The Irish lawyer whom I had seen was weary of the case, and would willingly have given up the property, without further ado, to a man who appeared to claim them; but on laying his tables and trees before my uncle, the latter had foreseen so many possible prior claimants, that the lawyer had begged him to undertake the management of the whole business. In his youth, my uncle would have liked nothing better than going over to Ireland himself, and ferreting out every scrap of paper or parchment, and every word of tradition respecting the family. As it was, old and gouty, he deputed me.

Accordingly, I went to Kildoon. I suspect I had something of my uncle's delight in following up a genealogical scent, for I very soon found out, when on the spot, that Mr. Rooney, the Irish lawyer, would have got both himself and the first claimant into a terrible scrape, if he had pronounced his opinion that the estates ought to be given up to him. There were three poor Irish fellows, each nearer of kin to the last possessor; but, a generation before, there was a still nearer relation, who had never been accounted for, nor his existence ever discovered by the lawyers, I venture to think, till I routed him out from the memory of some of the old dependants of the family. What had become of him? I travelled backwards and forwards; I crossed over to France, and came back again with a slight clue, which ended in my discovering that, wild and dissipated himself, he had left one child, a son, of yet worse character than his father; that this same Hugh Fitzgerald had married a very beautiful serving-woman of the Byrnes—a person below him in hereditary rank, but above him in character; that he had died soon after his marriage, leaving one child, whether a boy or a girl I could not learn, and that the mother had returned to live in the family of the Byrnes.

Now, the chief of this latter family was serving in the Duke of Berwick's regiment, and it was long before I could hear from him; it was more than a year before I got a short, haughty letter—I fancy he had a soldier's contempt for a civilian, an Irishman's hatred for an Englishman, an exiled Jacobite's jealousy of one who prospered and lived tranquilly under the government he looked upon as an usurpation. "Bridget Fitzgerald," he said, "had been faithful to the fortunes of his sister—had followed her abroad, and to England when Mrs. Starkey had thought fit to return. Both his sister and her husband were dead, he knew nothing of Bridget Fitzgerald at the present time: probably Sir Philip Tempest, his nephew's guardian, might be able to give me some information." I have not given the little contemptuous terms; the way in which faithful service was meant to imply more than it said—all that has nothing to do with my story. Sir Philip, when applied to, told me that he paid an annuity regularly to an old woman named Fitzgerald, living at Coldholme (the village near Starkey Manor-house). Whether she had any descendants he could not say.

One bleak March evening, I came in sight of the places described at the beginning of my story. I could hardly understand the rude dialect in which the direction to old Bridget's house was given.

"Yo' see yon furleets," all run together, gave me no idea that I was to guide myself by the distant lights that shone in the windows of the Hall, occupied for the time by a farmer who held the post of steward, while the Squire, now four or five and twenty, was making the grand tour. However, at last, I reached

Bridget's cottage—a low, moss-grown place: the palings that had once surrounded it were broken and gone; and the underwood of the forest came up to the walls, and must have darkened the windows. It was about seven o'clock—not late to my London notions—but, after knocking for some time at the door and receiving no reply, I was driven to conjecture that the occupant of the house was gone to bed. So I betook myself to the nearest church I had seen, three miles back on the road I had come, sure that close to that I should find an inn of some kind; and early the next morning I set off back to Coldholme, by a field-path which my host assured me I should find a shorter cut than the road I had taken the night before. It was a cold, sharp morning; my feet left prints in the sprinkling of hoar-frost that covered the ground; nevertheless, I saw an old woman, whom I instinctively suspected to be the object of my search, in a sheltered covert on one side of my path. I lingered and watched her. She must have been considerably above the middle size in her prime, for when she raised herself from the stooping position in which I first saw her, there was something fine and commanding in the erectness of her figure. She drooped again in a minute or two, and seemed looking for something on the ground, as, with bent head, she turned off from the spot where I gazed upon her, and was lost to my sight. I fancy I missed my way, and made a round in spite of the landlord's directions; for by the time I had reached Bridget's cottage she was there, with no semblance of hurried walk or discomposure of any kind. The door was slightly ajar. I knocked, and the majestic figure stood before me, silently awaiting the explanation of my errand. Her teeth were all gone, so the nose and chin were brought near together; the gray eyebrows were straight, and almost hung over her deep,

22

cavernous eyes, and the thick white hair lay in silvery masses over the low, wide, wrinkled forehead. For a moment, I stood uncertain how to shape my answer to the solemn questioning of her silence.

"Your name is Bridget Fitzgerald, I believe?"

She bowed her head in assent.

"I have something to say to you. May I come in? I am unwilling to keep you standing."

"You cannot tire me," she said, and at first she seemed inclined to deny me the shelter of her roof. But the next moment—she had searched the very soul in me with her eyes during that instant—she led me in, and dropped the shadowing hood of her gray, draping cloak, which had previously hid part of the character of her countenance. The cottage was rude and bare enough. But before the picture of the Virgin, of which I have made mention, there stood a little cup filled with fresh primroses. While she paid her reverence to the Madonna, I understood why she had been out seeking through the clumps of green in the sheltered copse. Then she turned round, and bade me be seated. The expression of her face, which all this time I was studying, was not bad, as the stories of my last night's landlord had led me to expect; it was a wild, stern, fierce, indomitable countenance, seamed and scarred by agonies of solitary weeping; but it was neither cunning nor malignant.

"My name is Bridget Fitzgerald," said she, by way of opening our conversation.

"And your husband was Hugh Fitzgerald, of Knock Mahon, near Kildoon, in Ireland?"

A faint light came into the dark gloom of her eyes.

"He was."

"May I ask if you had any children by him?"

The light in her eyes grew quick and red. She tried to speak, I could see; but something rose in her throat, and choked her, and until she could speak calmly, she would fain not speak at all before a stranger. In a minute or so she said—"I had a daughter—one Mary Fitzgerald,"—then her strong nature mastered her strong will, and she cried out, with a trembling wailing cry: "Oh, man! what of her?—what of her?"

She rose from her seat, and came and clutched at my arm, and looked in my eyes. There she read, as I suppose, my utter ignorance of what had become of her child; for she went blindly back to her chair, and sat rocking herself and softly moaning, as if I were not there; I not daring to speak to the lone and awful woman. After a little pause, she knelt down before the picture of Our Lady of the Holy Heart, and spoke to her by all the fanciful and poetic names of the Litany.

"O Rose of Sharon! O Tower of David! O Star of the Sea! have ye no comfort for my sore heart? Am I for ever to hope? Grant me at least despair!"—and so on she went, heedless of my presence. Her prayers grew wilder and wilder, till they seemed to me to touch on the borders of madness and blasphemy. Almost involuntarily, I spoke as if to stop her.

24

"Have you any reason to think that your daughter is dead?"

She rose from her knees, and came and stood before me.

"Mary Fitzgerald is dead," said she. "I shall never see her again in the flesh. No tongue ever told me; but I know she is dead. I have yearned so to see her, and my heart's will is fearful and strong: it would have drawn her to me before now, if she had been a wanderer on the other side of the world. I wonder often it has not drawn her out of the grave to come and stand before me, and hear me tell her how I loved her. For, sir, we parted unfriends."

I knew nothing but the dry particulars needed for my lawyer's quest, but I could not help feeling for the desolate woman; and she must have read the unusual sympathy with her wistful eyes.

"Yes, sir, we did. She never knew how I loved her; and we parted unfriends; and I fear me that I wished her voyage might not turn out well, only meaning,—O, blessed Virgin! you know I only meant that she should come home to her mother's arms as to the happiest place on earth; but my wishes are terrible—their power goes beyond my thought—and there is no hope for me, if my words brought Mary harm."

"But," I said, "you do not know that she is dead. Even now, you hoped she might be alive. Listen to me," and I told her the tale I have already told you, giving it all in the driest manner, for I wanted to recall the clear sense that I felt almost sure she had possessed in her younger days, and by keeping up her attention to details, restrain the vague wildness of her grief.

She listened with deep attention, putting from time to time such questions as convinced me I had to do with no common intelligence, however dimmed and shorn by solitude and mysterious sorrow. Then she took up her tale; and in few brief words, told me of her wanderings abroad in vain search after her daughter; sometimes in the wake of armies, sometimes in camp, sometimes in city. The lady, whose waiting-woman Mary had gone to be, had died soon after the date of her last letter home; her husband, the foreign officer, had been serving in Hungary, whither Bridget had followed him, but too late to find him. Vague rumours reached her that Mary had made a great marriage: and this sting of doubt was added,—whether the mother might not be close to her child under her new name, and even hearing of her every day; and yet never recognizing the lost one under the appellation she then bore. At length the thought took possession of her, that it was possible that all this time Mary might be at home at Coldholme, in the Trough of Bolland, in Lancashire, in England; and home came Bridget, in that vain hope, to her desolate hearth, and empty cottage. Here she had thought it safest to remain; if Mary was in life, it was here she would seek for her mother.

I noted down one or two particulars out of Bridget's narrative that I thought might be of use to me: for I was stimulated to further search in a strange and extraordinary manner. It seemed as if it were impressed upon me, that I must take up the quest where Bridget had laid it down; and this for no reason that had previously influenced me (such as my uncle's anxiety on the subject, my own reputation as a lawyer, and so on), but from some strange power which had taken possession of my will only that very morning, and which forced it in the direction it chose.

"I will go," said I. "I will spare nothing in the search. Trust to me. I will learn all that can be learnt. You shall know all that money, or pains, or wit can discover. It is true she may be long dead: but she may have left a child."

"A child!" she cried, as if for the first time this idea had struck her mind. "Hear him, Blessed Virgin! he says she may have left a child. And you have never told me, though I have prayed so for a sign, waking or sleeping!"

"Nay," said I, "I know nothing but what you tell me. You say you heard of her marriage."

But she caught nothing of what I said. She was praying to the Virgin in a kind of ecstasy, which seemed to render her unconscious of my very presence.

From Coldholme I went to Sir Philip Tempest's. The wife of the foreign officer had been a cousin of his father's, and from him I thought I might gain some particulars as to the existence of the Count de la Tour d'Auvergne, and where I could find him; for I knew questions de vive voix aid the flagging recollection, and I was determined to lose no chance for want of trouble. But Sir Philip had gone abroad, and it would be some time before I could receive an answer. So I followed my uncle's advice, to whom I had mentioned how wearied I felt, both in body and mind, by my will-o'-the-wisp search. He immediately told me to go to Harrogate, there to await Sir Philip's reply. I should be near to one of the places connected with my search, Coldholme; not far from Sir Philip Tempest, in case he returned, and I wished to ask him any further questions; and, in conclusion, my uncle bade me try to forget all about my business for a time.

This was far easier said than done. I have seen a child on a common blown along by a high wind, without power of standing still and resisting the tempestuous force. I was somewhat in the same predicament as regarded my mental state. Something resistless seemed to urge my thoughts on, through every possible course by which there was a chance of attaining to my object. I did not see the sweeping moors when I walked out: when I held a book in my hand, and read the words, their sense did not penetrate to my brain. If I slept, I went on with the same ideas, always flowing in the same direction. This could not last long without having a bad effect on the body. I had an illness, which, although I was racked with pain, was a positive relief to me, as it compelled me to live in the present suffering, and not in the visionary researches I had been continually making before. My kind uncle came to nurse me; and after the immediate danger was over, my life seemed to slip away in delicious languor for two or three months. I did not ask—so much did I dread falling into the old channel of thought—whether any reply had been received to my letter to Sir Philip. I turned my whole imagination right away from all that subject. My uncle remained with me until nigh midsummer, and then returned to his business in London; leaving me perfectly well, although not completely strong. I was to follow him in a fortnight; when, as he said, "we would look over letters, and talk about several things." I knew what this little speech alluded to, and shrank from the train of thought it suggested, which was so intimately connected with my first feelings of illness. However, I had a fortnight more to roam on those invigorating Yorkshire moors.

In those days, there was one large, rambling inn, at Harrogate, close to the Medicinal Spring; but it was already becoming too small for the accommodation of the influx of visitors, and many lodged round about, in the farm-houses of the district. It was so early in the season, that I had the inn pretty much to myself; and, indeed, felt rather like a visitor in a private house, so intimate had the landlord and landlady become with me during my long illness. She would chide me for being out so late on the moors, or for having been too long without food, quite in a motherly way; while he consulted me about vintages and wines, and taught me many a Yorkshire wrinkle about horses. In my walks I met other strangers from time to time. Even before my uncle had left me, I had noticed, with half-torpid curiosity, a young lady of very striking appearance, who went about always accompanied by an elderly companion,—hardly a gentlewoman, but with something in her look that prepossessed me in her favour. The younger lady always put her veil down when any one approached; so it had been only once or twice, when I had come upon her at a sudden turn in the path, that I had even had a glimpse at her face. I am not sure if it was beautiful, though in after-life I grew to think it so. But it was at this time overshadowed by a sadness that never varied: a pale, quiet, resigned look of intense suffering, that irresistibly attracted me,—not with love, but with a sense of infinite compassion for one so young yet so hopelessly unhappy. The companion wore something of the same look: quiet melancholy, hopeless, yet resigned. I asked my landlord who they were. He said they were called Clarke, and wished to be considered as mother and daughter; but that, for his part, he did not believe that to be their right name, or that there was any such relationship between them. They had been in the neighbourhood of Harrogate for some time, lodging in a remote farm-house. The people there would tell nothing about them; saying that they paid handsomely, and never did any harm; so why should they be speaking of any strange things that might happen? That, as the landlord shrewdly observed, showed there was something out of the common way he had heard that the elderly woman was a cousin of the farmer's where they lodged, and so the regard existing between relations might help to keep them quiet.

"What did he think, then, was the reason for their extreme seclusion?" asked I.

"Nay, he could not tell,—not he. He had heard that the young lady, for all as quiet as she seemed, played strange pranks at times." He shook his head when I asked him for more particulars, and refused to give them, which made me doubt if he knew any, for he was in general a talkative and communicative man. In default of other interests, after my uncle left, I set myself to watch these two people. I hovered about their walks drawn towards them with a strange fascination, which was not diminished by their evident annoyance at so frequently meeting me. One day, I had the sudden good fortune to be at hand when they were alarmed by the attack of a bull, which, in those unenclosed grazing districts, was a particularly dangerous occurrence. I have other and more important things to relate, than to tell of the accident which gave me an opportunity of rescuing them, it is enough to say, that this event was the beginning of an acquaintance, reluctantly acquiesced in by them, but eagerly prosecuted by me. I can hardly tell when intense curiosity became merged in love, but in less than ten days after my uncle's departure I was passionately enamoured of Mistress Lucy, as her attendant called her; carefully—for this I noted well—avoiding any address which appeared as if there was an equality of station between them. I noticed also that Mrs. Clarke, the elderly woman, after her first reluctance to allow me to pay them any attentions had been overcome, was cheered by my evident attachment to the young girl; it seemed to lighten her heavy burden of care, and she evidently favoured my visits to the farmhouse where they lodged. It was not so with Lucy. A more attractive person I never saw, in spite of her depression of manner, and shrinking avoidance of me. I felt sure at once, that whatever was the source of her grief, it rose from no fault of her own. It was difficult to draw her into conversation; but when at times, for a moment or two, I beguiled her into talk, I could see a rare intelligence in her face, and a grave, trusting look in the soft, gray eyes that were raised for a minute to mine. I made every excuse I possibly could for going there. I sought wild flowers for Lucy's sake; I planned walks for Lucy's sake; I watched the heavens by night, in hopes that some unusual beauty of sky would justify me in tempting Mrs. Clarke and Lucy forth upon the moors, to gaze at the great purple dome above.

It seemed to me that Lucy was aware of my love; but that, for some motive which I could not guess, she would fain have repelled me; but then again I saw, or fancied I saw, that her heart spoke in my favour, and that there was a struggle going on in her mind, which at times (I loved so dearly) I could have begged her to spare herself, even though the happiness of my whole life should have been the sacrifice; for her complexion grew paler, her aspect of sorrow more hopeless, her delicate frame yet slighter. During this period I had written, I should say, to my uncle, to beg to be allowed to prolong my stay at Harrogate, not giving any reason; but such was his tenderness towards me, that in a few days I heard from him, giving me a willing permission, and only charging me to take care of myself, and not use too much exertion during the hot weather.

One sultry evening I drew near the farm. The windows of their parlour were open, and I heard voices when I turned the corner of the house, as I passed the first window (there were two windows in their little ground-floor room). I saw Lucy distinctly; but when I had knocked at their door—the house-door stood always ajar—she was gone, and I saw only Mrs. Clarke, turning over the work-things lying on the table, in a nervous and purposeless manner. I felt by instinct that a conversation of some importance was coming on, in which I should be expected to say what was my object in paying these frequent visits. I was glad of the opportunity. My uncle had several times alluded to the pleasant possibility of my bringing home a young wife, to cheer and adorn the old house in Ormond Street. He was rich, and I was to succeed him, and had, as I knew, a fair reputation for so young a lawyer. So on my side I saw no obstacle. It was true that Lucy was shrouded in mystery; her name (I was convinced it was not Clarke), birth, parentage, and previous life were unknown to me. But I was sure of her goodness and sweet innocence, and although I knew that there must be something painful to be told, to account for her mournful sadness, yet I was willing to bear my share in her grief, whatever it might be.

Mrs. Clarke began, as if it was a relief to her to plunge into the subject.

"We have thought, sir—at least I have thought—that you knew very little of us, nor we of you, indeed; not enough to warrant the intimate acquaintance we have fallen into. I beg your pardon, sir," she went on, nervously; "I am but a plain kind of woman, and I mean to use no rudeness; but I must say straight out that I—we—think it would be better for you not to come so often to see us. She is very unprotected, and—"

"Why should I not come to see you, dear madam?" asked I, eagerly, glad of the opportunity of explaining myself. "I come, I own, because I have learnt to love Mistress Lucy, and wish to teach her to love me."

Mistress Clarke shook her head, and sighed.

"Don't, sir—neither love her, nor, for the sake of all you hold sacred, teach her to love you! If I am too late, and you love her already, forget her,—forget these last few weeks. O! I should never have allowed you to come!" she went on passionately; "but what am I to do? We are forsaken by all, except the great God, and even He permits a strange and evil power to afflict us—what am I to do! Where is it to end?" She wrung her hands in her distress; then she turned to me: "Go away, sir! go away, before you learn to care any more for her. I ask it for your own sake—I implore! You have been good and kind to us, and we shall always recollect you with gratitude; but go away now, and never come back to cross our fatal path!"

"Indeed, madam," said I, "I shall do no such thing. You urge it

33

for my own sake. I have no fear, so urged—nor wish, except to hear more—all. I cannot have seen Mistress Lucy in all the intimacy of this last fortnight, without acknowledging her goodness and innocence; and without seeing—pardon me, madam—that for some reason you are two very lonely women, in some mysterious sorrow and distress. Now, though I am not powerful myself, yet I have friends who are so wise and kind that they may be said to possess power. Tell me some particulars. Why are you in grief—what is your secret—why are you here? I declare solemnly that nothing you have said has daunted me in my wish to become Lucy's husband; nor will I shrink from any difficulty that, as such an aspirant, I may have to encounter. You say you are friendless—why cast away an honest friend? I will tell you of people to whom you may write, and who will answer any questions as to my character and prospects. I do not shun inquiry."

She shook her head again. "You had better go away, sir. You know nothing about us."

"I know your names," said I, "and I have heard you allude to the part of the country from which you came, which I happen to know as a wild and lonely place. There are so few people living in it that, if I chose to go there, I could easily ascertain all about you; but I would rather hear it from yourself." You see I wanted to pique her into telling me something definite.

"You do not know our true names, sir," said she, hastily.

"Well, I may have conjectured as much. But tell me, then, I conjure you. Give me your reasons for distrusting my willingness to stand by what I have said with regard to Mistress Lucy."

"Oh, what can I do?" exclaimed she. "If I am turning away a true friend, as he says?—Stay!" coming to a sudden decision—"I will tell you something—I cannot tell you all—you would not believe it. But, perhaps, I can tell you enough to prevent your going on in your hopeless attachment. I am not Lucy's mother."

"So I conjectured," I said. "Go on."

"I do not even know whether she is the legitimate or illegitimate child of her father. But he is cruelly turned against her; and her mother is long dead; and for a terrible reason, she has no other creature to keep constant to her but me. She—only two years ago—such a darling and such a pride in her father's house! Why, sir, there is a mystery that might happen in connection with her any moment; and then you would go away like all the rest; and, when you next heard her name, you would loathe her. Others, who have loved her longer, have done so before now. My poor child! whom neither God nor man has mercy upon—or, surely, she would die!"

The good woman was stopped by her crying. I confess, I was a little stunned by her last words; but only for a moment. At any rate, till I knew definitely what was this mysterious stain upon one so simple and pure, as Lucy seemed, I would not desert her, and so I said; and she made me answer:—

"If you are daring in your heart to think harm of my child, sir, after knowing her as you have done, you are no good man yourself; but I am so foolish and helpless in my great sorrow, that I would fain hope to find a friend in you. I cannot help trusting that, although you may no longer feel toward her as a lover, you will have pity upon us; and perhaps, by your learning you can tell us where to go for aid."

"I implore you to tell me what this mystery is," I cried, almost maddened by this suspense.

"I cannot," said she, solemnly. "I am under a deep vow of secrecy. If you are to be told, it must be by her." She left the room, and I remained to ponder over this strange interview. I mechanically turned over the few books, and with eyes that saw nothing at the time, examined the tokens of Lucy's frequent presence in that room.

When I got home at night, I remembered how all these trifles spoke of a pure and tender heart and innocent life. Mistress Clarke returned; she had been crying sadly.

"Yes," said she, "it is as I feared: she loves you so much that she is willing to run the fearful risk of telling you all herself—she acknowledges it is but a poor chance; but your sympathy will be a balm, if you give it. To-morrow, come here at ten in the morning; and, as you hope for pity in your hour of agony, repress all show of fear or repugnance you may feel towards one so grievously afflicted."

I half smiled. "Have no fear," I said. It seemed too absurd to imagine my feeling dislike to Lucy.

"Her father loved her well," said she, gravely, "yet he drove her out like some monstrous thing."

Just at this moment came a peal of ringing laughter from the garden. It was Lucy's voice; it sounded as if she were standing just on one side of the open casement—and as though she were suddenly stirred to merriment—merriment verging on boisterousness, by the doings or sayings of some other person. I can scarcely say why, but the sound jarred on me inexpressibly. She knew the subject of our conversation, and must have been at least aware of the state of agitation her friend was in; she herself usually so gentle and quiet. I half rose to go to the window, and satisfy my instinctive curiosity as to what had provoked this burst of, ill-timed laughter; but Mrs. Clarke threw her whole weight and power upon the hand with which she pressed and kept me down.

"For God's sake!" she said, white and trembling all over, "sit still; be quiet. Oh! be patient. To-morrow you will know all. Leave us, for we are all sorely afflicted. Do not seek to know more about us."

Again that laugh—so musical in sound, yet so discordant to my heart. She held me tight—tighter; without positive violence I could not have risen. I was sitting with my back to the window, but I felt a shadow pass between the sun's warmth and me, and a strange shudder ran through my frame. In a minute or two she released me.

"Go," repeated she. "Be warned, I ask you once more. I do not think you can stand this knowledge that you seek. If I had had my own way, Lucy should never have yielded, and promised to tell you all. Who knows what may come of it?"

"I am firm in my wish to know all. I return at ten to-morrow morning, and then expect to see Mistress Lucy herself."

I turned away; having my own suspicions, I confess, as to Mistress Clarke's sanity.

Conjectures as to the meaning of her hints, and uncomfortable thoughts connected with that strange laughter, filled my mind. I could hardly sleep. I rose early; and long before the hour I had appointed, I was on the path over the common that led to the old farm-house where they lodged. I suppose that Lucy had passed no better a night than I; for there she was also, slowly pacing with her even step, her eyes bent down, her whole look most saintly and pure. She started when I came close to her, and grew paler as I reminded her of my appointment, and spoke with something of the impatience of obstacles that, seeing her once more, had called up afresh in my mind. All strange and terrible hints, and giddy merriment were forgotten. My heart gave forth words of fire, and my tongue uttered them. Her colour went and came, as she listened; but, when I had ended my passionate speeches, she lifted her soft eyes to me, and said—

"But you know that you have something to learn about me yet. I only want to say this: I shall not think less of you—less well of you, I mean—if you, too, fall away from me when you know all. Stop!" said she, as if fearing another burst of mad words. "Listen to me. My father is a man of great wealth. I never knew my mother; she must have died when I was very young. When first I remember anything, I was living in a great, lonely house, with my dear and faithful Mistress Clarke. My father, even, was not there; he was—he is—a soldier, and his duties lie aboard.

38

But he came from time to time, and every time I think he loved me more and more. He brought me rarities from foreign lands, which prove to me now how much he must have thought of me during his absences. I can sit down and measure the depth of his lost love now, by such standards as these. I never thought whether he loved me or not, then; it was so natural, that it was like the air I breathed. Yet he was an angry man at times, even then; but never with me. He was very reckless, too; and, once or twice, I heard a whisper among the servants that a doom was over him, and that he knew it, and tried to drown his knowledge in wild activity, and even sometimes, sir, in wine. So I grew up in this grand mansion, in that lonely place. Everything around me seemed at my disposal, and I think every one loved me; I am sure I loved them. Till about two years ago—I remember it well—my father had come to England, to us; and he seemed so proud and so pleased with me and all I had done. And one day his tongue seemed loosened with wine, and he told me much that I had not known till then,—how dearly he had loved my mother, yet how his wilful usage had caused her death; and then he went on to say how he loved me better than any creature on earth, and how, some day, he hoped to take me to foreign places, for that he could hardly bear these long absences from his only child. Then he seemed to change suddenly, and said, in a strange, wild way, that I was not to believe what he said; that there was many a thing he loved better—his horse—his dog—I know not what.

"And 'twas only the next morning that, when I came into his room to ask his blessing as was my wont, he received me with fierce and angry words. 'Why had I,' so he asked, 'been delighting myself in such wanton mischief—dancing over the tender plants in the flower-beds, all set with the famous Dutch bulbs he had brought from Holland?' I had never been out of doors that morning, sir, and I could not conceive what he meant, and so I said; and then he swore at me for a liar, and said I was of no true blood, for he had seen me doing all that mischief himself—with his own eyes. What could I say? He would not listen to me, and even my tears seemed only to irritate him. That day was the beginning of my great sorrows. Not long after, he reproached me for my undue familiarity—all unbecoming a gentlewoman—with his grooms. I had been in the stable-yard, laughing and talking, he said. Now, sir, I am something of a coward by nature, and I had always dreaded horses; be-sides that, my father's servants—those whom he brought with him from foreign parts—were wild fellows, whom I had always avoided, and to whom I had never spoken, except as a lady must needs from time to time speak to her father's people. Yet my father called me by names of which I hardly know the meaning, but my heart told me they were such as shame any modest woman; and from that day he turned quite against me;—nay, sir, not many weeks after that, he came in with a riding-whip in his hand; and, accusing me harshly of evil doings, of which I knew no more than you, sir, he was about to strike me, and I, all in bewildering tears, was ready to take his stripes as great kindness compared to his harder words, when suddenly he stopped his arm mid-way, gasped and staggered, crying out, 'The curse—the curse!' I looked up in terror. In the great mirror opposite I saw myself, and right behind, another wicked, fearful self, so like me that my soul seemed to quiver within me, as though not knowing to which similitude of body it belonged. My father saw

40

my double at the same moment, either in its dreadful reality, whatever that might be, or in the scarcely less terrible reflection in the mirror; but what came of it at that moment I cannot say, for I suddenly swooned away; and when I came to myself I was lying in my bed, and my faithful Clarke sitting by me. I was in my bed for days; and even while I lay there my double was seen by all, flitting about the house and gardens, always about some mischievous or detestable work. What wonder that every one shrank from me in dread—that my father drove me forth at length, when the disgrace of which I was the cause was past his patience to bear. Mistress Clarke came with me; and here we try to live such a life of piety and prayer as may in time set me free from the curse."

All the time she had been speaking, I had been weighing her story in my mind. I had hitherto put cases of witchcraft on one side, as mere superstitions; and my uncle and I had had many an argument, he supporting himself by the opinion of his good friend Sir Matthew Hale. Yet this sounded like the tale of one bewitched; or was it merely the effect of a life of extreme seclusion telling on the nerves of a sensitive girl? My scepticism inclined me to the latter belief, and when she paused I said:

"I fancy that some physician could have disabused your father of his belief in visions—"

Just at that instant, standing as I was opposite to her in the full and perfect morning light, I saw behind her another figure—a ghastly resemblance, complete in likeness, so far as form and feature and minutest touch of dress could go, but with a loathsome demon soul looking out of the gray eyes, that were in turns mocking and voluptuous. My heart stood still within me; every hair rose up erect; my flesh crept with horror. I could not see the grave and tender Lucy—my eyes were fascinated by the creature beyond. I know not why, but I put out my hand to clutch it; I grasped nothing but empty air, and my whole blood curdled to ice. For a moment I could not see; then my sight came back, and I saw Lucy standing before me, alone, deathly pale, and, I could have fancied, almost, shrunk in size.

"It has been near me?" she said, as if asking a question.

The sound seemed taken out of her voice; it was husky as the notes on an old harpsichord when the strings have ceased to vibrate. She read her answer in my face, I suppose, for I could not speak. Her look was one of intense fear, but that died away into an aspect of most humble patience. At length she seemed to force herself to face behind and around her: she saw the purple moors, the blue distant hills, quivering in the sunlight, but nothing else.

"Will you take me home?" she said, meekly.

I took her by the hand, and led her silently through the budding heather—we dared not speak; for we could not tell but that the dread creature was listening, although unseen,—but that IT might appear and push us asunder. I never loved her more fondly than now when—and that was the unspeakable misery— the idea of her was becoming so inextricably blended with the shuddering thought of IT. She seemed to understand what I must be feeling. She let go my hand, which she had kept clasped until then, when we reached the garden gate, and went forwards to meet her anxious friend, who was standing by the window looking for her. I could not enter the house: I needed silence, society, leisure, change—I knew not what—to shake off the sensation of that creature's presence. Yet I lingered about the garden—I hardly know why; I partly suppose, because I feared to encounter the resemblance again on the solitary common, where it had vanished, and partly from a feeling of inexpressible compassion for Lucy. In a few minutes Mistress Clarke came forth and joined me. We walked some paces in silence.

"You know all now," said she, solemnly.

"I saw IT," said I, below my breath.

"And you shrink from us, now," she said, with a hopelessness which stirred up all that was brave or good in me.

"Not a whit," said I. "Human flesh shrinks from encounter with the powers of darkness: and, for some reason unknown to me, the pure and holy Lucy is their victim."

"The sins of the fathers shall be visited upon the children," she said.

"Who is her father?" asked I. "Knowing as much as I do, I may surely know more—know all. Tell me, I entreat you, madam, all that you can conjecture respecting this demoniac persecution of one so good."

"I will; but not now. I must go to Lucy now. Come this afternoon, I will see you alone; and oh, sir! I will trust that you may yet find some way to help us in our sore trouble!"

I was miserably exhausted by the swooning affright which had taken possession of me. When I reached the inn, I staggered in like one overcome by wine. I went to my own private room. It was some time before I saw that the weekly post had come in, and brought me my letters. There was one from my uncle, one from my home in Devonshire, and one, re-directed over the first address, sealed with a great coat of arms, It was from Sir Philip Tempest: my letter of inquiry respecting Mary Fitzgerald had reached him at Liége, where it so happened that the Count de la Tour d'Auvergne was quartered at the very time. He remembered his wife's beautiful attendant; she had had high words with the deceased countess, respecting her intercourse with an English gentleman of good standing, who was also in the foreign service. The countess augured evil of his intentions; while Mary, proud and vehement, asserted that he would soon marry her, and resented her mistress's warnings as an insult. The consequence was, that she had left Madame de la Tour d'Auvergne's service, and, as the Count believed, had gone to live with the Englishman; whether he had married her, or not, he could not say. "But," added Sir Philip Tempest, "you may easily hear what particulars you wish to know respecting Mary Fitzgerald from the Englishman himself, if, as I suspect, he is no other than my neighbour and former acquaintance, Mr. Gisborne, of Skipford Hall, in the West Riding. I am led to the belief that he is no other, by several small particulars, none of which are in themselves conclusive, but which, taken together, furnish a mass of presumptive evidence. As far as I could make out from the Count's foreign pronunciation, Gisborne was the name of the Englishman: I know that Gisborne of Skipford was abroad and in the foreign service at that time—he was a likely fellow enough for such an exploit, and, above all, certain expressions recur to my mind which he used in reference to old Bridget Fitzgerald, of Coldholme, whom he once encountered while staying with me at Starkey Manor-house. I remember that the meeting seemed to have produced some extraordinary effect upon his mind, as though he had suddenly discovered some connection which she might have had with his previous life. I beg you to let me know if I can be of any further service to you. Your uncle once rendered me a good turn, and I will gladly repay it, so far as in me lies, to his nephew."

I was now apparently close on the discovery which I had striven so many months to attain. But success had lost its zest. I put my letters down, and seemed to forget them all in thinking of the morning I had passed that very day. Nothing was real but the unreal presence, which had come like an evil blast across my bodily eyes, and burnt itself down upon my brain. Dinner came, and went away untouched. Early in the afternoon I walked to the farm-house. I found Mistress Clarke alone, and I was glad and relieved. She was evidently prepared to tell me all I might wish to hear.

"You asked me for Mistress Lucy's true name; it is Gisborne," she began.

"Not Gisborne of Skipford?" I exclaimed, breathless with anticipation.

"The same," said she, quietly, not regarding my manner. "Her father is a man of note; although, being a Roman Catholic, he cannot take that rank in this country to which his station entitles him. The consequence is that he lives much abroad—has been a soldier, I am told."

"And Lucy's mother?" I asked.

She shook her head. "I never knew her," said she. "Lucy was about three years old when I was engaged to take charge of her. Her mother was dead."

"But you know her name?—you can tell if it was Mary Fitzgerald?"

She looked astonished. "That was her name. But, sir, how came you to be so well acquainted with it? It was a mystery to the whole household at Skipford Court. She was some beautiful young woman whom he lured away from her protectors while he was abroad. I have heard said he practised some terrible deceit upon her, and when she came to know it, she was neither to have nor to hold, but rushed off from his very arms, and threw herself into a rapid stream and was drowned. It stung him deep with remorse, but I used to think the remembrance of the mother's cruel death made him love the child yet dearer."

I told her, as briefly as might be, of my researches after the descendant and heir of the Fitzgeralds of Kildoon, and added— something of my old lawyer spirit returning into me for the moment—that I had no doubt but that we should prove Lucy to be by right possessed of large estates in Ireland.

No flush came over her gray face; no light into her eyes. "And what is all the wealth in the whole world to that poor girl?" she said. "It will not free her from the ghastly bewitchment which persecutes her. As for money, what a pitiful thing it is! it cannot touch her."

"No more can the Evil Creature harm her," I said. "Her holy nature dwells apart, and cannot be defiled or stained by all the devilish arts in the whole world."

"True! but it is a cruel fate to know that all shrink from her, sooner or later, as from one possessed — accursed."

"How came it to pass?" I asked.

"Nay, I know not. Old rumours there are, that were bruited through the household at Skipford."

"Tell me," I demanded.

"They came from servants, who would fain account for every thing. They say that, many years ago, Mr. Gisborne killed a dog belonging to an old witch at Coldholme; that she cursed, with a dreadful and mysterious curse, the creature, whatever it might be, that he should love best; and that it struck so deeply into his heart that for years he kept himself aloof from any temptation to love aught. But who could help loving Lucy?"

"You never heard the witch's name?" I gasped.

"Yes — they called her Bridget: they said he would never go near the spot again for terror of her. Yet he was a brave man!"

"Listen," said I, taking hold of her arm, the better to arrest her full attention: "if what I suspect holds true, that man stole Bridget's only child — the very Mary Fitzgerald who was Lucy's mother; if so, Bridget cursed him in ignorance of the deeper

47

wrong he had done her. To this hour she yearns after her lost child, and questions the saints whether she be living or not. The roots of that curse lie deeper than she knows: she unwittingly banned him for a deeper guilt than that of killing a dumb beast. The sins of the fathers are indeed visited upon the children."

"But," said Mistress Clarke, eagerly, "she would never let evil rest on her own grandchild? Surely, sir, if what you say be true, there are hopes for Lucy. Let us go—go at once, and tell this fearful woman all that you suspect, and beseech her to take off the spell she has put upon her innocent grandchild."

It seemed to me, indeed, that something like this was the best course we could pursue. But first it was necessary to ascertain more than what mere rumour or careless hearsay could tell. My thoughts turned to my uncle—he could advise me wisely—he ought to know all. I resolved to go to him without delay; but I did not choose to tell Mistress Clarke of all the visionary plans that flitted through my mind. I simply declared my intention of proceeding straight to London on Lucy's affairs. I bade her believe that my interest on the young lady's behalf was greater than ever, and that my whole time should be given up to her cause. I saw that Mistress Clarke distrusted me, because my mind was too full of thoughts for my words to flow freely. She sighed and shook her head, and said, "Well, it is all right!" in such a tone that it was an implied reproach. But I was firm and constant in my heart, and I took confidence from that.

I rode to London. I rode long days drawn out into the lovely summer nights: I could not rest. I reached London. I told my uncle all, though in the stir of the great city the horror had faded away, and I could hardly imagine that he would believe the account I gave him of the fearful double of Lucy which I had seen on the lonely moor-side. But my uncle had lived many years, and learnt many things; and, in the deep secrets of family history that had been confided to him, he had heard of cases of innocent people bewitched and taken possession of by evil spirits yet more fearful than Lucy's. For, as he said, to judge from all I told him, that resemblance had no power over her— she was too pure and good to be tainted by its evil, haunting presence. It had, in all probability, so my uncle conceived, tried to suggest wicked thoughts and to tempt to wicked actions but she, in her saintly maidenhood, had passed on undefiled by evil thought or deed. It could not touch her soul: but true, it set her apart from all sweet love or common human intercourse. My uncle threw himself with an energy more like six-and-twenty than sixty into the consideration of the whole case. He undertook the proving Lucy's descent, and volunteered to go and find out Mr. Gisborne, and obtain, firstly, the legal proofs of her descent from the Fitzgeralds of Kildoon, and, secondly, to try and hear all that he could respecting the working of the curse, and whether any and what means had been taken to exorcise that terrible appearance. For he told me of instances where, by prayers and long fasting, the evil possessor had been driven forth with howling and many cries from the body which it had come to inhabit; he spoke of those strange New England cases which had happened not so long before; of Mr. Defoe, who had written a book, wherein he had named many modes of subduing apparitions, and sending them back whence they came; and, lastly, he spoke low of dreadful ways of compelling witches to undo their witchcraft. But I could not endure to hear of those

49

tortures and burnings. I said that Bridget was rather a wild and savage woman than a malignant witch; and, above all, that Lucy was of her kith and kin; and that, in putting her to the trial, by water or by fire, we should be torturing—it might be to the death—the ancestress of her we sought to redeem.

My uncle thought awhile, and then said, that in this last matter I was right—at any rate, it should not be tried, with his consent, till all other modes of remedy had failed; and he assented to my proposal that I should go myself and see Bridget, and tell her all.

In accordance with this, I went down once more to the wayside inn near Coldholme. It was late at night when I arrived there; and, while I supped, I inquired of the landlord more particulars as to Bridget's ways. Solitary and savage had been her life for many years. Wild and despotic were her words and manner to those few people who came across her path. The country-folk did her imperious bidding, because they feared to disobey. If they pleased her, they prospered; if, on the contrary, they neglected or traversed her behests, misfortune, small or great, fell on them and theirs. It was not detestation so much as an indefinable terror that she excited.

In the morning I went to see her. She was standing on the green outside her cottage, and received me with the sullen grandeur of a throneless queen. I read in her face that she recognized me, and that I was not unwelcome; but she stood silent till I had opened my errand.

"I have news of your daughter," said I, resolved to speak straight to all that I knew she felt of love, and not to spare her. "She is dead!"

50

The stern figure scarcely trembled, but her hand sought the support of the door-post.

"I knew that she was dead," said she, deep and low, and then was silent for an instant. "My tears that should have flowed for her were burnt up long years ago. Young man, tell me about her."

"Not yet," said I, having a strange power given me of confronting one, whom, nevertheless, in my secret soul I dreaded.

"You had once a little dog," I continued. The words called out in her more show of emotion than the intelligence of her daughter's death. She broke in upon my speech:—

"I had! It was hers—the last thing I had of hers—and it was shot for wantonness! It died in my arms. The man who killed that dog rues it to this day. For that dumb beast's blood, his best-beloved stands accursed."

Her eyes distended, as if she were in a trance and saw the working of her curse. Again I spoke:—

"O, woman!" I said, "that best-beloved, standing accursed before men, is your dead daughter's child."

The life, the energy, the passion, came back to the eyes with which she pierced through me, to see if I spoke truth; then, without another question or word, she threw herself on the ground with fearful vehemence, and clutched at the innocent daisies with convulsed hands.

51

"Bone of my bone! flesh of my flesh! have I cursed thee — and art thou accursed?"

So she moaned, as she lay prostrate in her great agony. I stood aghast at my own work. She did not hear my broken sentences; she asked no more, but the dumb confirmation which my sad looks had given that one fact, that her curse rested on her own daughter's child. The fear grew on me lest she should die in her strife of body and soul; and then might not Lucy remain under the spell as long as she lived?

Even at this moment, I saw Lucy coming through the woodland path that led to Bridget's cottage; Mistress Clarke was with her: I felt at my heart that it was she, by the balmy peace which the look of her sent over me, as she slowly advanced, a glad surprise shining out of her soft quiet eyes. That was as her gaze met mine. As her looks fell on the woman lying stiff, convulsed on the earth, they became full of tender pity; and she came forward to try and lift her up. Seating herself on the turf, she took Bridget's head into her lap; and, with gentle touches, she arranged the dishevelled gray hair streaming thick and wild from beneath her mutch.

"God help her!" murmured Lucy. "How she suffers!"

At her desire we sought for water; but when we returned, Bridget had recovered her wandering senses, and was kneeling with clasped hands before Lucy, gazing at that sweet sad face as though her troubled nature drank in health and peace from every moment's contemplation. A faint tinge on Lucy's pale cheeks showed me that she was aware of our return; otherwise it appeared as if she was conscious of her influence for good over the passionate and troubled woman kneeling before her, and would not willingly avert her grave and loving eyes from that wrinkled and careworn countenance.

Suddenly—in the twinkling of an eye—the creature appeared, there, behind Lucy; fearfully the same as to outward semblance, but kneeling exactly as Bridget knelt, and clasping her hands in jesting mimicry as Bridget clasped hers in her ecstasy that was deepening into a prayer. Mistress Clarke cried out—Bridget arose slowly, her gaze fixed on the creature beyond: drawing her breath with a hissing sound, never moving her terrible eyes, that were steady as stone, she made a dart at the phantom, and caught, as I had done, a mere handful of empty air. We saw no more of the creature—it vanished as suddenly as it came, but Bridget looked slowly on, as if watching some receding form. Lucy sat still, white, trembling, drooping—I think she would have swooned if I had not been there to uphold her. While I was attending to her, Bridget passed us, without a word to any one, and, entering her cottage, she barred herself in, and left us without.

All our endeavours were now directed to get Lucy back to the house where she had tarried the night before. Mistress Clarke told me that, not hearing from me (some letter must have miscarried), she had grown impatient and despairing, and had urged Lucy to the enterprise of coming to seek her grandmother; not telling her, indeed, of the dread reputation she possessed, or how we suspected her of having so fearfully blighted that innocent girl; but, at the same time, hoping much from the mysterious stirring of blood, which Mistress Clarke trusted in for the removal of the curse. They had come, by a different route from that which I had taken, to a village inn not far from Coldholme, only the night before. This was the first interview between ancestress and descendant.

All through the sultry noon I wandered along the tangled brush-wood of the old neglected forest, thinking where to turn for remedy in a matter so complicated and mysterious. Meeting a countryman, I asked my way to the nearest clergyman, and went, hoping to obtain some counsel from him. But he proved to be a coarse and common-minded man, giving no time or attention to the intricacies of a case, but dashing out a strong opinion involving immediate action. For instance, as soon as I named Bridget Fitzgerald, he exclaimed:—

"The Coldholme witch! the Irish papist! I'd have had her ducked long since but for that other papist, Sir Philip Tempest. He has had to threaten honest folk about here over and over again, or they'd have had her up before the justices for her black doings. And it's the law of the land that witches should be burnt! Ay, and of Scripture, too, sir! Yet you see a papist, if he's a rich squire, can overrule both law and Scripture. I'd carry a faggot myself to rid the country of her!"

Such a one could give me no help. I rather drew back what I had already said; and tried to make the parson forget it, by treating him to several pots of beer, in the village inn, to which we had adjourned for our conference at his suggestion. I left him as soon as I could, and returned to Coldholme, shaping my way past deserted Starkey Manor-house, and coming upon it by the back. At that side were the oblong remains of the old moat, the waters of which lay placid and motionless under the crimson rays of the setting sun; with the forest-trees lying straight along each side, and their deep-green foliage mirrored to blackness in the burnished surface of the moat below—and the broken sun-dial at the end nearest the hall—and the heron, standing on one leg at the water's edge, lazily looking down for fish—the lonely and desolate house scarce needed the broken windows, the weeds on the door-sill, the broken shutter softly flapping to and fro in the twilight breeze, to fill up the picture of desertion and decay. I lingered about the place until the growing darkness warned me on. And then I passed along the path, cut by the orders of the last lady of Starkey Manor-House, that led me to Bridget's cottage. I resolved at once to see her; and, in spite of closed doors—it might be of resolved will—she should see me. So I knocked at her door, gently, loudly, fiercely. I shook it so vehemently that a length the old hinges gave way, and with a crash it fell inwards, leaving me suddenly face to face with Bridget—I, red, heated, agitated with my so long baffled efforts—she, stiff as any stone, standing right facing me, her eyes dilated with terror, her ashen lips trembling, but her body motionless. In her hands she held her crucifix, as if by that holy symbol she sought to oppose my entrance. At sight of me, her whole frame relaxed, and she sank back upon a chair. Some mighty tension had given way. Still her eyes looked fearfully into the gloom of the outer air, made more opaque by the glimmer of the lamp inside, which she had placed before the picture of the Virgin.

"Is she there?" asked Bridget, hoarsely.

"No! Who? I am alone. You remember me."

55

"Yes," replied she, still terror stricken. "But she—that creature—has been looking in upon me through that window all day long. I closed it up with my shawl; and then I saw her feet below the door, as long as it was light, and I knew she heard my very breathing—nay, worse, my very prayers; and I could not pray, for her listening choked the words ere they rose to my lips. Tell me, who is she?—what means that double girl I saw this morning? One had a look of my dead Mary; but the other curdled my blood, and yet it was the same!"

She had taken hold of my arm, as if to secure herself some human companionship. She shook all over with the slight, never-ceasing tremor of intense terror. I told her my tale as I have told it you, sparing none of the details.

How Mistress Clarke had informed me that the resemblance had driven Lucy forth from her father's house—how I had disbelieved, until, with mine own eyes, I had seen another Lucy standing behind my Lucy, the same in form and feature, but with the demon-soul looking out of the eyes. I told her all, I say, believing that she—whose curse was working so upon the life of her innocent grandchild—was the only person who could find the remedy and the redemption. When I had done, she sat silent for many minutes.

"You love Mary's child?" she asked.

"I do, in spite of the fearful working of the curse—I love her. Yet I shrink from her ever since that day on the moor-side. And men must shrink from one so accompanied; friends and lovers must stand afar off. Oh, Bridget Fitzgerald! loosen the curse! Set her free!"

"Where is she?"

I eagerly caught at the idea that her presence was needed, in order that, by some strange prayer or exorcism, the spell might be reversed.

"I will go and bring her to you," I exclaimed. Bridget tightened her hold upon my arm.

"Not so," said she, in a low, hoarse voice. "It would kill me to see her again as I saw her this morning. And I must live till I have worked my work. Leave me!" said she, suddenly, and again taking up the cross. "I defy the demon I have called up. Leave me to wrestle with it!"

She stood up, as if in an ecstasy of inspiration, from which all fear was banished. I lingered—why I can hardly tell—until once more she bade me begone. As I went along the forest way, I looked back, and saw her planting the cross in the empty threshold, where the door had been.

The next morning Lucy and I went to seek her, to bid her join her prayers with ours. The cottage stood open and wide to our gaze. No human being was there: the cross remained on the threshold, but Bridget was gone.

CHAPTER III

What was to be done next? was the question that I asked myself. As for Lucy, she would fain have submitted to the doom that lay upon her. Her gentleness and piety, under the pressure of so horrible a life, seemed over-passive to me. She never complained. Mrs. Clarke complained more than ever. As for me, I was more in love with the real Lucy than ever; but I shrunk from the false similitude with an intensity proportioned to my love. I found out by instinct that Mrs. Clarke had occasional temptations to leave Lucy. The good lady's nerves were shaken, and, from what she said, I could almost have concluded that the object of the Double was to drive away from Lucy this last, and almost earliest friend. At times, I could scarcely bear to own it, but I myself felt inclined to turn recreant; and I would accuse Lucy of being too patient—too resigned. One after another, she won the little children of Coldholme. (Mrs. Clarke and she had resolved to stay there, for was it not as good a place as any other, to such as they? and did not all our faint hopes rest on Bridget— never seen or heard of now, but still we trusted to come back, or give some token?) So, as I say, one after another, the little children came about my Lucy, won by her soft tones, and her gentle smiles, and kind actions. Alas! one after another they fell away, and shrunk from her path with blanching terror; and we too surely guessed the reason why. It was the last drop. I could bear it no longer. I resolved no more to linger around the spot, but to go back to my uncle, and among the learned divines of the city of London, seek for some power whereby to annul the curse.

My uncle, meanwhile, had obtained all the requisite testimonials relating to Lucy's descent and birth, from the Irish lawyers, and from Mr. Gisborne. The latter gentleman had written from abroad (he was again serving in the Austrian army), a letter alternately passionately self-reproachful and stoically repellant. It was evident that when he thought of Mary—her short life—how he had wronged her, and of her violent death, he could hardly find words severe enough for his own conduct; and from this point of view, the curse that Bridget had laid upon him and his, was regarded by him as a prophetic doom, to the utterance of which she was moved by a Higher Power, working for the fulfilment of a deeper vengeance than for the death of the poor dog. But then, again, when he came to speak of his daughter, the repugnance which the conduct of the demoniac creature had produced in his mind, was but ill-disguised under a show of profound indifference as to Lucy's fate. One almost felt as if he would have been as content to put her out of existence, as he would have been to destroy some disgusting reptile that had invaded his chamber or his couch.

The great Fitzgerald property was Lucy's; and that was all—was nothing.

My uncle and I sat in the gloom of a London November evening, in our house in Ormond Street. I was out of health, and felt as if I were in an inextricable coil of misery. Lucy and I wrote to each other, but that was little; and we dared not see each other for dread of the fearful Third, who had more than once taken her place at our meetings. My uncle had, on the day I speak of, bidden prayers to be put up on the ensuing Sabbath in many a church and meeting-house in London, for one grievously tormented by an evil spirit. He had faith in prayers—I had none; I was fast losing faith in all things. So we sat, he trying to interest me in the old talk of other days, I oppressed by one thought—when our old servant, Anthony, opened the door, and, without speaking, showed in a very gentlemanly and prepossessing man, who had something remarkable about his dress, betraying his profession to be that of the Roman Catholic priesthood. He glanced at my uncle first, then at me. It was to me he bowed.

"I did not give my name," said he, "because you would hardly have recognised it; unless, sir, when, in the north, you heard of Father Bernard, the chaplain at Stoney Hurst?"

I remembered afterwards that I had heard of him, but at the time I had utterly forgotten it; so I professed myself a complete stranger to him; while my ever-hospitable uncle, although hating a papist as much as it was in his nature to hate anything, placed a chair for the visitor, and bade Anthony bring glasses, and a fresh jug of claret.

Father Bernard received this courtesy with the graceful ease and pleasant acknowledgement which belongs to a man of the world. Then he turned to scan me with his keen glance. After some alight conversation, entered into on his part, I am certain, with an intention of discovering on what terms of confidence I stood with my uncle, he paused, and said gravely—

"I am sent here with a message to you, sir, from a woman to whom you have shown kindness, and who is one of my penitents, in Antwerp—one Bridget Fitzgerald."

60

"Bridget Fitzgerald!" exclaimed I. "In Antwerp? Tell me, sir, all that you can about her."

"There is much to be said," he replied. "But may I inquire if this gentleman — if your uncle is acquainted with the particulars of which you and I stand informed?"

"All that I know, he knows," said I, eagerly laying my hand on my uncle's arm, as he made a motion as if to quit the room.

"Then I have to speak before two gentlemen who, however they may differ from me in faith, are yet fully impressed with the fact that there are evil powers going about continually to take cognizance of our evil thoughts: and, if their Master gives them power, to bring them into overt action. Such is my theory of the nature of that sin, which I dare not disbelieve — as some sceptics would have us do — the sin of witchcraft. Of this deadly sin, you and I are aware, Bridget Fitzgerald has been guilty. Since you saw her last, many prayers have been offered in our churches, many masses sung, many penances undergone, in order that, if God and the holy saints so willed it, her sin might be blotted out. But it has not been so willed."

"Explain to me," said I, "who you are, and how you come connected with Bridget. Why is she at Antwerp? I pray you, sir, tell me more. If I am impatient, excuse me; I am ill and feverish, and in consequence bewildered."

There was something to me inexpressibly soothing in the tone of voice with which he began to narrate, as it were from the beginning, his acquaintance with Bridget.

61

"I had known Mr. and Mrs. Starkey during their residence abroad, and so it fell out naturally that, when I came as chaplain to the Sherburnes at Stoney Hurst, our acquaintance was renewed; and thus I became the confessor of the whole family, isolated as they were from the offices of the Church, Sherburne being their nearest neighbour who professed the true faith. Of course, you are aware that facts revealed in confession are sealed as in the grave; but I learnt enough of Bridget's character to be convinced that I had to do with no common woman; one powerful for good as for evil. I believe that I was able to give her spiritual assistance from time to time, and that she looked upon me as a servant of that Holy Church, which has such wonderful power of moving men's hearts, and relieving them of the burden of their sins. I have known her cross the moors on the wildest nights of storm, to confess and be absolved; and then she would return, calmed and subdued, to her daily work about her mistress, no one witting where she had been during the hours that most passed in sleep upon their beds. After her daughter's departure—after Mary's mysterious disappearance—I had to impose many a long penance, in order to wash away the sin of impatient repining that was fast leading her into the deeper guilt of blasphemy. She set out on that long journey of which you have possibly heard—that fruitless journey in search of Mary— and during her absence, my superiors ordered my return to my former duties at Antwerp, and for many years I heard no more of Bridget.

"Not many months ago, as I was passing homewards in the evening, along one of the streets near St. Jacques, leading into the Meer Straet, I saw a woman sitting crouched up under the shrine of the Holy Mother of Sorrows. Her hood was drawn over her head, so that the shadow caused by the light of the lamp above fell deep over her face; her hands were clasped round her knees. It was evident that she was some one in hopeless trouble, and as such it was my duty to stop and speak. I naturally addressed her first in Flemish, believing her to be one of the lower class of inhabitants. She shook her head, but did not look up. Then I tried French, and she replied in that language, but speaking it so indifferently, that I was sure she was either English or Irish, and consequently spoke to her in my own native tongue. She recognized my voice; and, starting up, caught at my robes, dragging me before the blessed shrine, and throwing herself down, and forcing me, as much by her evident desire as by her action, to kneel beside her, she exclaimed:

"'O Holy Virgin! you will never hearken to me again, but hear him; for you know him of old, that he does your bidding, and strives to heal broken hearts. Hear him!'

"She turned to me.

"'She will hear you, if you will only pray. She never hears me: she and all the saints in heaven cannot hear my prayers, for the Evil One carries them off, as he carried that first away. O, Father Bernard, pray for me!'

"I prayed for one in sore distress, of what nature I could not say; but the Holy Virgin would know. Bridget held me fast, gasping with eagerness at the sound of my words. When I had ended, I rose, and, making the sign of the Cross over her, I was going to bless her in the name of the Holy Church, when she shrank away like some terrified creature, and said —

63

"'I am guilty of deadly sin, and am not shriven.'

"'Arise, my daughter,' said I, 'and come with me.' And I led the way into one of the confessionals of St. Jaques.

"She knelt; I listened. No words came. The evil powers had stricken her dumb, as I heard afterwards they had many a time before, when she approached confession.

"She was too poor to pay for the necessary forms of exorcism; and hitherto those priests to whom she had addressed herself were either so ignorant of the meaning of her broken French, or her Irish-English, or else esteemed her to be one crazed—as, indeed, her wild and excited manner might easily have led any one to think—that they had neglected the sole means of loosening her tongue, so that she might confess her deadly sin, and, after due penance, obtain absolution. But I knew Bridget of old, and felt that she was a penitent sent to me. I went through those holy offices appointed by our Church for the relief of such a case. I was the more bound to do this, as I found that she had come to Antwerp for the sole purpose of discovering me, and making confession to me. Of the nature of that fearful confession I am forbidden to speak. Much of it you know; possibly all.

"It now remains for her to free herself from mortal guilt, and to set others free from the consequences thereof. No prayers, no masses, will ever do it, although they may strengthen her with that strength by which alone acts of deepest love and purest self-devotion may be performed. Her words of passion, and cries for revenge—her unholy prayers could never reach the ears of the holy saints! Other powers intercepted them, and wrought so

64

that the curses thrown up to heaven have fallen on her own flesh and blood; and so, through her very strength of love, have brused and crushed her heart. Henceforward her former self must be buried,—yea, buried quick, if need be,—but never more to make sign, or utter cry on earth! She has become a Poor Clare, in order that, by perpetual penance and constant service of others, she may at length so act as to obtain final absolution and rest for her soul. Until then, the innocent must suffer. It is to plead for the innocent that I come to you; not in the name of the witch, Bridget Fitzgerald, but of the penitent and servant of all men, the Poor Clare, Sister Magdalen."

"Sir," said I, "I listen to your request with respect; only I may tell you it is not needed to urge me to do all that I can on behalf of one, love for whom is part of my very life. If for a time I have absented myself from her, it is to think and work for her redemption. I, a member of the English Church—my uncle, a Puritan—pray morning and night for her by name: the congregations of London, on the next Sabbath, will pray for one unknown, that she may be set free from the Powers of Darkness. Moreover, I must tell you, sir, that those evil ones touch not the great calm of her soul. She lives her own pure and loving life, unharmed and untainted, though all men fall off from her. I would I could have her faith!"

My uncle now spoke.

"Nephew," said he, "it seems to me that this gentleman, although professing what I consider an erroneous creed, has touched upon the right point in exhorting Bridget to acts of love and mercy, whereby to wipe out her sin of hate and vengeance.

Let us strive after our fashion, by almsgiving and visiting of the needy and fatherless, to make our prayers acceptable. Meanwhile, I myself will go down into the north, and take charge of the maiden. I am too old to be daunted by man or demon. I will bring her to this house as to a home; and let the Double come if it will! A company of godly divines shall give it the meeting, and we will try issue."

The kindly, brave old man! But Father Bernard sat on musing.

"All hate," said he, "cannot be quenched in her heart; all Christian forgiveness cannot have entered into her soul, or the demon would have lost its power. You said, I think, that her grandchild was still tormented?"

"Still tormented!" I replied, sadly, thinking of Mistress Clarke's last letter—He rose to go. We afterwards heard that the occasion of his coming to London was a secret political mission on behalf of the Jacobites. Nevertheless, he was a good and a wise man.

Months and months passed away without any change. Lucy entreated my uncle to leave her where she was,—dreading, as I learnt, lest if she came, with her fearful companion, to dwell in the same house with me, that my love could not stand the repeated shocks to which I should be doomed. And this she thought from no distrust of the strength of my affection, but from a kind of pitying sympathy for the terror to the nerves which she clearly observed that the demoniac visitation caused in all.

I was restless and miserable. I devoted myself to good works; but I performed them from no spirit of love, but solely from the

66

hope of reward and payment, and so the reward was never granted. At length, I asked my uncle's leave to travel; and I went forth, a wanderer, with no distincter end than that of many another wanderer—to get away from myself. A strange impulse led me to Antwerp, in spite of the wars and commotions then raging in the Low Countries—or rather, perhaps, the very craving to become interested in something external, led me into the thick of the struggle then going on with the Austrians. The cities of Flanders were all full at that time of civil disturbances and rebellions, only kept down by force, and the presence of an Austrian garrison in every place.

I arrived in Antwerp, and made inquiry for Father Bernard. He was away in the country for a day or two. Then I asked my way to the Convent of Poor Clares; but, being healthy and prosperous, I could only see the dim, pent-up, gray walls, shut closely in by narrow streets, in the lowest part of the town. My landlord told me, that had I been stricken by some loathsome disease, or in desperate case of any kind, the Poor Clares would have taken me, and tended me. He spoke of them as an order of mercy of the strictest kind, dressing scantily in the coarsest materials, going barefoot, living on what the inhabitants of Antwerp chose to bestow, and sharing even those fragments and crumbs with the poor and helpless that swarmed all around; receiving no letters or communication with the outer world; utterly dead to everything but the alleviation of suffering. He smiled at my inquiring whether I could get speech of one of them; and told me that they were even forbidden to speak for the purposes of begging their daily food; while yet they lived, and fed others upon what was given in charity.

"But," exclaimed I, "supposing all men forgot them! Would they quietly lie down and die, without making sign of their extremity?"

"If such were the rule the Poor Clares would willingly do it; but their founder appointed a remedy for such extreme cases as you suggest. They have a bell—'tis but a small one, as I have heard, and has yet never been rung in the memory man: when the Poor Clares have been without food for twenty-four hours, they may ring this bell, and then trust to our good people of Antwerp for rushing to the rescue of the Poor Clares, who have taken such blessed care of us in all our straits."

It seemed to me that such rescue would be late in the day; but I did not say what I thought. I rather turned the conversation, by asking my landlord if he knew, or had ever heard, anything of a certain Sister Magdalen.

"Yes," said he, rather under his breath, "news will creep out, even from a convent of Poor Clares. Sister Magdalen is either a great sinner or a great saint. She does more, as I have heard, than all the other nuns put together; yet, when last month they would fain have made her mother-superior, she begged rather that they would place her below all the rest, and make her the meanest servant of all."

"You never saw her?" asked I.

"Never," he replied.

I was weary of waiting for Father Bernard, and yet I lingered in Antwerp. The political state of things became worse than ever, increased to its height by the scarcity of food consequent on many deficient harvests. I saw groups of fierce, squalid men, at every corner of the street, glaring out with wolfish eyes at my sleek skin and handsome clothes.

At last Father Bernard returned. We had a long conversation, in which he told me that, curiously enough, Mr. Gisborne, Lucy's father, was serving in one of the Austrian regiments, then in garrison at Antwerp. I asked Father Bernard if he would make us acquainted; which he consented to do. But, a day or two afterwards, he told me that, on hearing my name, Mr. Gisborne had declined responding to any advances on my part, saying he had adjured his country, and hated his countrymen.

Probably he recollected my name in connection with that of his daughter Lucy. Anyhow, it was clear enough that I had no chance of making his acquaintance. Father Bernard confirmed me in my suspicions of the hidden fermentation, for some coming evil, working among the "blouses" of Antwerp, and he would fain have had me depart from out the city; but I rather craved the excitement of danger, and stubbornly refused to leave.

One day, when I was walking with him in the Place Verte, he bowed to an Austrian officer, who was crossing towards the cathedral.

"That is Mr. Gisborne," said he, as soon as the gentleman was past.

I turned to look at the tall, slight figure of the officer. He carried himself in a stately manner, although he was past middle age, and from his years might have had some excuse for a slight stoop. As I looked at the man, he turned round, his eyes met mine, and I saw his face. Deeply lined, sallow, and scathed was that countenance; scarred by passion as well as by the fortunes of war. 'Twas but a moment our eyes met. We each turned round, and went on our separate way.

But his whole appearance was not one to be easily forgotten; the thorough appointment of the dress, and evident thought bestowed on it, made but an incongruous whole with the dark, gloomy expression of his countenance. Because he was Lucy's father, I sought instinctively to meet him everywhere. At last he must have become aware of my pertinacity, for he gave me a haughty scowl whenever I passed him. ¡ In one of these encounters, however, I chanced to be of some service to him. He was turning the corner of a street, and came suddenly on one of the groups of discontented Flemings of whom I have spoken. Some words were exchanged, when my gentleman out with his sword, and with a slight but skilful cut drew blood from one of those who had insulted him, as he fancied, though I was too far off to hear the words. They would all have fallen upon him had I not rushed forwards and raised the cry, then well known in Antwerp, of rally, to the Austrian soldiers who were perpetually patrolling the streets, and who came in numbers to the rescue. I think that neither Mr. Gisborne nor the mutinous group of plebeians owed me much gratitude for my interference. He had planted himself against a wall, in a skilful attitude of fence, ready with his bright glancing rapier to do battle with all the heavy, fierce, unarmed men, some six or seven in number. But when his own soldiers came up, he sheathed his sword; and, giving some careless word of command, sent them away again, and continued his saunter all alone down the street, the workmen snarling in his rear, and more than half-inclined to fall on me for my cry for rescue. I cared not if they did, my life seemed so dreary a burden just then; and, perhaps, it was this daring loitering among them that prevented their attacking me. Instead, they suffered me to fall into conversation with them; and I heard some of their grievances. Sore and heavy to be borne were they, and no wonder the sufferers were savage and desperate.

The man whom Gisborne had wounded across his face would fain have got out of me the name of his aggressor, but I refused to tell it. Another of the group heard his inquiry, and made answer — "I know the man. He is one Gisborne, aide-de-camp to the General-Commandant. I know him well."

He began to tell some story in connection with Gisborne in a low and muttering voice; and while he was relating a tale, which I saw excited their evil blood, and which they evidently wished me not to hear, I sauntered away and back to my lodgings.

That night Antwerp was in open revolt. The inhabitants rose in rebellion against their Austrian masters. The Austrians, holding the gates of the city, remained at first pretty quiet in the citadel; only, from time to time, the boom of the great cannon swept sullenly over the town. But if they expected the disturbance to die away, and spend itself in a few hours' fury, they were mistaken. In a day or two, the rioters held possession of the principal municipal buildings. Then the Austrians poured forth in bright flaming array, calm and smiling, as they marched to the posts assigned, as if the fierce mob were no more to them then

71

the swarms of buzzing summer flies. Their practised manœuvres, their well-aimed shot, told with terrible effect; but in the place of one slain rioter, three sprang up of his blood to avenge his loss. But a deadly foe, a ghastly ally of the Austrians, was at work. Food, scarce and dear for months, was now hardly to be obtained at any price. Desperate efforts were being made to bring provisions into the city, for the rioters had friends without. Close to the city port, nearest to the Scheldt, a great struggle took place. I was there, helping the rioters, whose cause I had adopted. We had a savage encounter with the Austrians. Numbers fell on both sides: I saw them lie bleeding for a moment: then a volley of smoke obscured them; and when it cleared away, they were dead—trampled upon or smothered, pressed down and hidden by the freshly-wounded whom those last guns had brought low. And then a gray-robed and grey-veiled figure came right across the flashing guns and stooped over some one, whose life-blood was ebbing away; sometimes it was to give him drink from cans which they carried slung at their sides; sometimes I saw the cross held above a dying man, and rapid prayers were being uttered, unheard by men in that hellish din and clangour, but listened to by One above. I saw all this as in a dream: the reality of that stern time was battle and carnage. But I knew that these gray figures, their bare feet all wet with blood, and their faces hidden by their veils, were the Poor Clares—sent forth now because dire agony was abroad and imminent danger at hand. Therefore, they left their cloistered shelter, and came into that thick and evil mêlée.

Close to me—driven past me by the struggle of many fighters— came the Antwerp burgess with the scarce-healed scar upon his face; and in an instant more, he was thrown by the press upon the Austrian officer Gisborne, and ere either had recovered the shock, the burgess had recognized his opponent.

"Ha! the Englishman Gisborne!" he cried, and threw himself upon him with redoubled fury. He had struck him hard—the Englishman was down; when out of the smoke came a dark-gray figure, and threw herself right under the uplifted flashing sword. The burgess's arm stood arrested. Neither Austrians nor Anversois willingly harmed the Poor Clares.

"Leave him to me!" said a low stern voice. "He is mine enemy—mine for many years."

Those words were the last I heard. I myself was struck down by a bullet. I remember nothing more for days. When I came to myself, I was at the extremity of weakness, and was craving for food to recruit my strength. My landlord sat watching me. He, too, looked pinched and shrunken; he had heard of my wounded state, and sought me out. Yes! the struggle still continued, but the famine was sore: and some, he had heard, had died for lack of food. The tears stood in his eyes as he spoke. But soon he shook off his weakness, and his natural cheerfulness returned. Father Bernard had been to see me—no one else. (Who should, indeed?) Father Bernard would come back that afternoon—he had promised. But Father Bernard never came, although I was up and dressed, and looking eagerly for him.

My landlord brought me a meal which he had cooked himself: of what it was composed he would not say, but it was most excellent, and with every mouthful I seemed to gain strength. The good man sat looking at my evident enjoyment with a happy smile of sympathy; but, as my appetite became satisfied, I began to detect a certain wistfulness in his eyes, as if craving for the food I had so nearly devoured—for, indeed, at that time I was hardly aware of the extent of the famine. Suddenly, there was a sound of many rushing feet past our window. My landlord opened one of the sides of it, the better to learn what was going on. Then we heard a faint, cracked, tinkling bell, coming shrill upon the air, clear and distinct from all other sounds. "Holy Mother!" exclaimed my landlord, "the Poor Clares!"

He snatched up the fragments of my meal, and crammed them into my hands, bidding me follow. Down stairs he ran, clutching at more food, as the women of his house eagerly held it out to him; and in a moment we were in the street, moving along with the great current, all tending towards the Convent of the Poor Clares. And still, as if piercing our ears with its inarticulate cry, came the shrill tinkle of the bell. In that strange crowd were old men trembling and sobbing, as they carried their little pittance of food; women with tears running down their cheeks, who had snatched up what provisions they had in the vessels in which they stood, so that the burden of these was in many cases much greater than that which they contained; children, with flushed faces, grasping tight the morsel of bitten cake or bread, in their eagerness to carry it safe to the help of the Poor Clares; strong men—yea, both Anversois and Austrians— pressing onward with set teeth, and no word spoken; and over all, and through all, came that sharp tinkle—that cry for help in extremity.

We met the first torrent of people returning with blanched and piteous faces: they were issuing out of the convent to make way for the offerings of others. "Haste, haste!" said they. "A Poor Clare is dying! A Poor Clare is dead for hunger! God forgive us and our city!"

We pressed on. The stream bore us along where it would. We were carried through refectories, bare and crumbless; into cells over whose doors the conventual name of the occupant was written. Thus it was that I, with others, was forced into Sister Magdalen's cell. On her couch lay Gisborne, pale unto death, but not dead. By his side was a cup of water, and a small morsel of mouldy bread, which he had pushed out of his reach, and could not move to obtain. Over against his bed were these words, copied in the English version "Therefore, if thine enemy hunger, feed him; if he thirst, give him drink."

Some of us gave him of our food, and left him eating greedily, like some famished wild animal. For now it was no longer the sharp tinkle, but that one solemn toll, which in all Christian countries tells of the passing of the spirit out of earthly life into eternity; and again a murmur gathered and grew, as of many people speaking with awed breath, "A Poor Clare is dying! a Poor Clare is dead!"

Borne along once more by the motion of the crowd, we were carried into the chapel belonging to the Poor Clares. On a bier before the high altar, lay a woman—lay Sister Magdalen—lay Bridget Fitzgerald. By her side stood Father Bernard, in his robes of office, and holding the crucifix on high while he pronounced the solemn absolution of the Church, as to one who had newly confessed herself of deadly sin. I pushed on with passionate force, till I stood close to the dying woman, as she received extreme unction amid the breathless and awed hush of the multitude around. Her eyes were glazing, her limbs were stiffening; but when the rite was over and finished, she raised her gaunt figure slowly up, and her eyes brightened to a strange intensity of joy, as, with the gesture of her finger and the trance-like gleam of her eye, she seemed like one who watched the disappearance of some loathed and fearful creature.

"She is freed from the curse!" said she, as she fell back dead.

THE DOOM OF THE GRIFFITHS

CHAPTER I

I have always been much interested by the traditions which are scattered up and down North Wales relating to Owen Glendower (Owain Glendwr is the national spelling of the name), and I fully enter into the feeling which makes the Welsh peasant still look upon him as the hero of his country. There was great joy among many of the inhabitants of the principality, when the subject of the Welsh prize poem at Oxford, some fifteen or sixteen years ago, was announced to be "Owain Glendwr." It was the most proudly national subject that had been given for years.

Perhaps, some may not be aware that this redoubted chieftain is, even in the present days of enlightenment, as famous among his illiterate countrymen for his magical powers as for his patriotism. He says himself—or Shakespeare says it for him, which is much the same thing—

> 'At my nativity
> The front of heaven was full of fiery shapes
> Of burning cressets . . .
> . . . I can call spirits from the vasty deep.'

And few among the lower orders in the principality would think of asking Hotspur's irreverent question in reply.

Among other traditions preserved relative to this part of the Welsh hero's character, is the old family prophecy which gives title to this tale. When Sir David Gam, "as black a traitor as if he had been born in Builth," sought to murder Owen at Machynlleth, there was one with him whose name Glendwr little dreamed of having associated with his enemies. Rhys ap Gryfydd, his "old familiar friend," his relation, his more than brother, had consented unto his blood. Sir David Gam might be forgiven, but one whom he had loved, and who had betrayed him, could never be forgiven. Glendwr was too deeply read in the human heart to kill him. No, he let him live on, the loathing and scorn of his compatriots, and the victim of bitter remorse. The mark of Cain was upon him.

But before he went forth—while he yet stood a prisoner, cowering beneath his conscience before Owain Glendwr—that chieftain passed a doom upon him and his race:

"I doom thee to live, because I know thou wilt pray for death. Thou shalt live on beyond the natural term of the life of man, the scorn of all good men. The very children shall point to thee with hissing tongue, and say, 'There goes one who would have shed a brother's blood!' For I loved thee more than a brother, oh Rhys ap Gryfydd! Thou shalt live on to see all of thy house, except the weakling in arms, perish by the sword. Thy race shall be accursed. Each generation shall see their lands melt away like snow; yea their wealth shall vanish, though they may labour night and day to heap up gold. And when nine generations have passed from the face of the earth, thy blood shall no longer flow in the veins of any human being. In those days the last male of thy race shall avenge me. The son shall slay the father."

Such was the traditionary account of Owain Glendwr's speech to his once-trusted friend. And it was declared that the doom had been fulfilled in all things; that live in as miserly a manner as they would, the Griffiths never were wealthy and prosperous—indeed that their worldly stock diminished without any visible cause.

But the lapse of many years had almost deadened the wonder-inspiring power of the whole curse. It was only brought forth from the hoards of Memory when some untoward event happened to the Griffiths family; and in the eighth generation the faith in the prophecy was nearly destroyed, by the marriage of the Griffiths of that day, to a Miss Owen, who, unexpectedly, by the death of a brother, became an heiress—to no considerable amount, to be sure, but enough to make the prophecy appear reversed. The heiress and her husband removed from his small patrimonial estate in Merionethshire, to her heritage in Caernarvonshire, and for a time the prophecy lay dormant.

If you go from Tremadoc to Criccaeth, you pass by the parochial church of Ynysynhanarn, situated in a boggy valley running from the mountains, which shoulder up to the Rivals, down to Cardigan Bay. This tract of land has every appearance of having been redeemed at no distant period of time from the sea, and has all the desolate rankness often attendant upon such marshes. But the valley beyond, similar in character, had yet more of gloom at the time of which I write. In the higher part there were large plantations of firs, set too closely to attain any size, and remaining stunted in height and scrubby in appearance. Indeed, many of the smaller and more weakly had died, and the bark had fallen down on the brown soil neglected and unnoticed. These trees had a ghastly appearance, with their white trunks, seen by the dim light which struggled through the thick boughs above. Nearer to the sea, the valley assumed a more open, though hardly a more cheerful character; it looked dark and overhung by sea-fog through the greater part of the year, and even a farm-house, which usually imparts something of cheerfulness to a landscape, failed to do so here. This valley formed the greater part of the estate to which Owen Griffiths became entitled by right of his wife. In the higher part of the valley was situated the family mansion, or rather dwelling-house, for "mansion" is too grand a word to apply to the clumsy, but substantially-built Bodowen. It was square and heavy-looking, with just that much pretension to ornament necessary to distinguish it from the mere farm-house.

In this dwelling Mrs. Owen Griffiths bore her husband two sons—Llewellyn, the future Squire, and Robert, who was early destined for the Church. The only difference in their situation, up to the time when Robert was entered at Jesus College, was, that the elder was invariably indulged by all around him, while Robert was thwarted and indulged by turns; that Llewellyn never learned anything from the poor Welsh parson, who was nominally his private tutor; while occasionally Squire Griffiths made a great point of enforcing Robert's diligence, telling him that, as he had his bread to earn, he must pay attention to his learning. There is no knowing how far the very irregular education he had received would have carried Robert through his college examinations; but, luckily for him in this respect, before such a trial of his learning came round, he heard of the death of his elder brother, after a short illness, brought on by a hard drinking-bout. Of course, Robert was summoned home, and it seemed quite as much of course, now that there was no necessity for him to "earn his bread by his learning," that he should not return to Oxford. So the half-educated, but not unintelligent, young man continued at home, during the short remainder of his parent's lifetime.

His was not an uncommon character. In general he was mild, indolent, and easily managed; but once thoroughly roused, his passions were vehement and fearful. He seemed, indeed, almost afraid of himself, and in common hardly dared to give way to justifiable anger—so much did he dread losing his self-control. Had he been judiciously educated, he would, probably, have distinguished himself in those branches of literature which call for taste and imagination, rather than any exertion of reflection or judgment. As it was, his literary taste showed itself in making collections of Cambrian antiquities of every description, till his stock of Welsh MSS. would have excited the envy of Dr. Pugh himself, had he been alive at the time of which I write.

There is one characteristic of Robert Griffiths which I have omitted to note, and which was peculiar among his class. He was no hard drinker; whether it was that his head was easily affected, or that his partially-refined taste led him to dislike intoxication and its attendant circumstances, I cannot say; but at five-and-twenty Robert Griffiths was habitually sober—a thing so rare in Llyn, that he was almost shunned as a churlish, unsociable being, and paused much of his time in solitude.

About this time, he had to appear in some case that was tried at the Caernarvon assizes; and while there, was a guest at the house of his agent, a shrewd, sensible Welsh attorney, with one daughter, who had charms enough to captivate Robert Griffiths. Though he remained only a few days at her father's house, they were sufficient to decide his affections, and short was the period allowed to elapse before he brought home a mistress to Bodowen. The new Mrs. Griffiths was a gentle, yielding person, full of love toward her husband, of whom, nevertheless, she stood something in awe, partly arising from the difference in their ages, partly from his devoting much time to studies of which she could understand nothing.

She soon made him the father of a blooming little daughter, called Augharad after her mother. Then there came several uneventful years in the household of Bodowen; and when the old women had one and all declared that the cradle would not rock again, Mrs. Griffiths bore the son and heir. His birth was soon followed by his mother's death: she had been ailing and low-spirited during her pregnancy, and she seemed to lack the buoyancy of body and mind requisite to bring her round after her time of trial. Her husband, who loved her all the more from having few other claims on his affections, was deeply grieved by her early death, and his only comforter was the sweet little boy whom she had left behind. That part of the squire's character, which was so tender, and almost feminine, seemed called forth by the helpless situation of the little infant, who stretched out his arms to his father with the same earnest cooing that happier children make use of to their mother alone. Augharad was almost neglected, while the little Owen was king of the house; still next to his father, none tended him so lovingly as his sister. She was so accustomed to give way to him that it was no longer a hardship. By night and by day Owen was the constant companion of his father, and increasing years seemed only to confirm the custom. It was an unnatural life for the child, seeing no bright little faces peering into his own (for Augharad was, as I said before, five or six years older, and her face, poor motherless girl! was often anything but bright), hearing no din of clear ringing voices, but day after day sharing the otherwise solitary hours of his father, whether in the dim room, surrounded by wizard-like antiquities, or pattering his little feet to keep up with his "tada" in his mountain rambles or shooting excursions. When the pair came to some little foaming brook, where the stepping-stones were far and wide, the father carried his little boy across with the tenderest care; when the lad was weary, they rested, he cradled in his father's arms, or the Squire would lift him up and carry him to his home again. The boy was indulged (for his father felt flattered by the desire) in his wish of sharing his meals and keeping the same hours. All this indulgence did not render Owen unamiable, but it made him wilful, and not a happy child. He had a thoughtful look, not common to the face of a young boy. He knew no games, no merry sports; his information was of an imaginative and speculative character. His father delighted to interest him in his own studies, without considering how far they were healthy for so young a mind.

Of course Squire Griffiths was not unaware of the prophecy

which was to be fulfilled in his generation. He would occasionally refer to it when among his friends, with sceptical levity; but in truth it lay nearer to his heart than he chose to acknowledge. His strong imagination rendered him peculiarly impressible on such subjects; while his judgment, seldom exercised or fortified by severe thought, could not prevent his continually recurring to it. He used to gaze on the half-sad countenance of the child, who sat looking up into his face with his large dark eyes, so fondly yet so inquiringly, till the old legend swelled around his heart, and became too painful for him not to require sympathy. Besides, the overpowering love he bore to the child seemed to demand fuller vent than tender words; it made him like, yet dread, to upbraid its object for the fearful contrast foretold. Still Squire Griffiths told the legend, in a half-jesting manner, to his little son, when they were roaming over the wild heaths in the autumn days, "the saddest of the year," or while they sat in the oak-wainscoted room, surrounded by mysterious relics that gleamed strangely forth by the flickering fire-light. The legend was wrought into the boy's mind, and he would crave, yet tremble, to hear it told over and over again, while the words were intermingled with caresses and questions as to his love. Occasionally his loving words and actions were cut short by his father's light yet bitter speech— "Get thee away, my lad; thou knowest not what is to come of all this love."

When Augharad was seventeen, and Owen eleven or twelve, the rector of the parish in which Bodowen was situated, endeavoured to prevail on Squire Griffiths to send the boy to school. Now, this rector had many congenial tastes with his parishioner, and was his only intimate; and, by repeated arguments, he succeeded in convincing the Squire that the unnatural life Owen was leading was in every way injurious. Unwillingly was the father wrought to part from his son; but he did at length send him to the Grammar School at Bangor, then under the management of an excellent classic. Here Owen showed that he had more talents than the rector had given him credit for, when he affirmed that the lad had been completely stupefied by the life he led at Bodowen. He bade fair to do credit to the school in the peculiar branch of learning for which it was famous. But he was not popular among his schoolfellows. He was wayward, though, to a certain degree, generous and unselfish; he was reserved but gentle, except when the tremendous bursts of passion (similar in character to those of his father) forced their way.

On his return from school one Christmas-time, when he had been a year or so at Bangor, he was stunned by hearing that the undervalued Augharad was about to be married to a gentleman of South Wales, residing near Aberystwith. Boys seldom appreciate their sisters; but Owen thought of the many slights with which he had requited the patient Augharad, and he gave way to bitter regrets, which, with a selfish want of control over his words, he kept expressing to his father, until the Squire was thoroughly hurt and chagrined at the repeated exclamations of "What shall we do when Augharad is gone?" "How dull we shall be when Augharad is married!" Owen's holidays were prolonged a few weeks, in order that he might be present at the wedding; and when all the festivities were over, and the bride and bridegroom had left Bodowen, the boy and his father really felt how much they missed the quiet, loving Augharad. She had performed so many thoughtful, noiseless little offices, on which their daily comfort depended; and now she was gone, the household seemed to miss the spirit that peacefully kept it in order; the servants roamed about in search of commands and directions, the rooms had no longer the unobtrusive ordering of taste to make them cheerful, the very fires burned dim, and were always sinking down into dull heaps of gray ashes. Altogether Owen did not regret his return to Bangor, and this also the mortified parent perceived. Squire Griffiths was a selfish parent.

Letters in those days were a rare occurrence. Owen usually received one during his half-yearly absences from home, and occasionally his father paid him a visit. This half-year the boy had no visit, nor even a letter, till very near the time of his leaving school, and then he was astounded by the intelligence that his father was married again.

Then came one of his paroxysms of rage; the more disastrous in its effects upon his character because it could find no vent in action. Independently of slight to the memory of the first wife which children are so apt to fancy such an action implies, Owen had hitherto considered himself (and with justice) the first object of his father's life. They had been so much to each other; and now a shapeless, but too real something had come between him and his father there for ever. He felt as if his permission should have been asked, as if he should have been consulted. Certainly he ought to have been told of the intended event. So the Squire felt, and hence his constrained letter which had so much increased the bitterness of Owen's feelings.

With all this anger, when Owen saw his stepmother, he thought he had never seen so beautiful a woman for her age; for she was no longer in the bloom of youth, being a widow when his father married her. Her manners, to the Welsh lad, who had seen little of female grace among the families of the few antiquarians with whom his father visited, were so fascinating that he watched her with a sort of breathless admiration. Her measured grace, her faultless movements, her tones of voice, sweet, till the ear was sated with their sweetness, made Owen less angry at his father's marriage. Yet he felt, more than ever, that the cloud was between him and his father; that the hasty letter he had sent in answer to the announcement of his wedding was not forgotten, although no allusion was ever made to it. He was no longer his father's confidant—hardly ever his father's companion, for the newly-married wife was all in all to the Squire, and his son felt himself almost a cipher, where he had so long been everything. The lady herself had ever the softest consideration for her stepson; almost too obtrusive was the attention paid to his wishes, but still he fancied that the heart had no part in the winning advances. There was a watchful glance of the eye that Owen once or twice caught when she had imagined herself unobserved, and many other nameless little circumstances, that gave him a strong feeling of want of sincerity in his stepmother. Mrs. Owen brought with her into the family her little child by her first husband, a boy nearly three years old. He was one of those elfish, observant, mocking children, over whose feelings you seem to have no control: agile and mischievous, his little practical jokes, at first performed in ignorance of the pain he gave, but afterward proceeding to a malicious pleasure in suffering, really seemed to afford some ground to the superstitious notion of some of the common people that he was a fairy changeling.

Years passed on; and as Owen grew older he became more observant. He saw, even in his occasional visits at home (for from school he had passed on to college), that a great change had taken place in the outward manifestations of his father's character; and, by degrees, Owen traced this change to the influence of his stepmother; so slight, so imperceptible to the common observer, yet so resistless in its effects. Squire Griffiths caught up his wife's humbly advanced opinions, and, unawares to himself, adopted them as his own, defying all argument and opposition. It was the same with her wishes; they met their fulfilment, from the extreme and delicate art with which she insinuated them into her husband's mind, as his own. She sacrificed the show of authority for the power. At last, when Owen perceived some oppressive act in his father's conduct toward his dependants, or some unaccountable thwarting of his own wishes, he fancied he saw his stepmother's secret influence thus displayed, however much she might regret the injustice of his father's actions in her conversations with him when they were alone. His father was fast losing his temperate habits, and frequent intoxication soon took its usual effect upon the temper. Yet even here was the spell of his wife upon him. Before her he placed a restraint upon his passion, yet she was perfectly aware of his irritable disposition, and directed it hither and thither with the same apparent ignorance of the tendency of her words.

Meanwhile Owen's situation became peculiarly mortifying to a youth whose early remembrances afforded such a contrast to his present state. As a child, he had been elevated to the

88

consequence of a man before his years gave any mental check to the selfishness which such conduct was likely to engender; he could remember when his will was law to the servants and dependants, and his sympathy necessary to his father: now he was as a cipher in his father's house; and the Squire, estranged in the first instance by a feeling of the injury he had done his son in not sooner acquainting him with his purposed marriage, seemed rather to avoid than to seek him as a companion, and too frequently showed the most utter indifference to the feelings and wishes which a young man of a high and independent spirit might be supposed to indulge.

Perhaps Owen was not fully aware of the force of all these circumstances; for an actor in a family drama is seldom unimpassioned enough to be perfectly observant. But he became moody and soured; brooding over his unloved existence, and craving with a human heart after sympathy.

This feeling took more full possession of his mind when he had left college, and returned home to lead an idle and purposeless life. As the heir, there was no worldly necessity for exertion: his father was too much of a Welsh squire to dream of the moral necessity, and he himself had not sufficient strength of mind to decide at once upon abandoning a place and mode of life which abounded in daily mortifications; yet to this course his judgment was slowly tending, when some circumstances occurred to detain him at Bodowen.

It was not to be expected that harmony would long be preserved, even in appearance, between an unguarded and soured young man, such as Owen, and his wary stepmother, when he had once left college, and come, not as a visitor, but as the heir to his father's house. Some cause of difference occurred, where the woman subdued her hidden anger sufficiently to become convinced that Owen was not entirely the dupe she had believed him to be. Henceforward there was no peace between them. Not in vulgar altercations did this show itself; but in moody reserve on Owen's part, and in undisguised and contemptuous pursuance of her own plans by his stepmother. Bodowen was no longer a place where, if Owen was not loved or attended to, he could at least find peace, and care for himself: he was thwarted at every step, and in every wish, by his father's desire, apparently, while the wife sat by with a smile of triumph on her beautiful lips.

So Owen went forth at the early day dawn, sometimes roaming about on the shore or the upland, shooting or fishing, as the season might be, but oftener "stretched in indolent repose" on the short, sweet grass, indulging in gloomy and morbid reveries. He would fancy that this mortified state of existence was a dream, a horrible dream, from which he should awake and find himself again the sole object and darling of his father. And then he would start up and strive to shake off the incubus. There was the molten sunset of his childish memory; the gorgeous crimson piles of glory in the west, fading away into the cold calm light of the rising moon, while here and there a cloud floated across the western heaven, like a seraph's wing, in its flaming beauty; the earth was the same as in his childhood's days, full of gentle evening sounds, and the harmonies of twilight—the breeze came sweeping low over the heather and blue-bells by his side, and the turf was sending up its evening incense of perfume. But life,

90

and heart, and hope were changed for ever since those bygone days!

Or he would seat himself in a favourite niche of the rocks on Moel Gêst, hidden by a stunted growth of the whitty, or mountain-ash, from general observation, with a rich-tinted cushion of stone-crop for his feet, and a straight precipice of rock rising just above. Here would he sit for hours, gazing idly at the bay below with its back-ground of purple hills, and the little fishing-sail on its bosom, showing white in the sunbeam, and gliding on in such harmony with the quiet beauty of the glassy sea; or he would pull out an old school-volume, his companion for years, and in morbid accordance with the dark legend that still lurked in the recesses of his mind—a shape of gloom in those innermost haunts awaiting its time to come forth in distinct outline—would he turn to the old Greek dramas which treat of a family foredoomed by an avenging Fate. The worn page opened of itself at the play of the Œdipus Tyrannus, and Owen dwelt with the craving disease upon the prophecy so nearly resembling that which concerned himself. With his consciousness of neglect, there was a sort of self-flattery in the consequence which the legend gave him. He almost wondered how they durst, with slights and insults, thus provoke the Avenger.

The days drifted onward. Often he would vehemently pursue some sylvan sport, till thought and feeling were lost in the violence of bodily exertion. Occasionally his evenings were spent at a small public-house, such as stood by the unfrequented wayside, where the welcome, hearty, though bought, seemed so strongly to contrast with the gloomy negligence of home—unsympathising home.

One evening (Owen might be four or five-and-twenty), wearied with a day's shooting on the Clenneny Moors, he passed by the open door of "The Goat" at Penmorfa. The light and the cheeriness within tempted him, poor self-exhausted man! as it has done many a one more wretched in worldly circumstances, to step in, and take his evening meal where at least his presence was of some consequence. It was a busy day in that little hostel. A flock of sheep, amounting to some hundreds, had arrived at Penmorfa, on their road to England, and thronged the space before the house. Inside was the shrewd, kind-hearted hostess, bustling to and fro, with merry greetings for every tired drover who was to pass the night in her house, while the sheep were penned in a field close by. Ever and anon, she kept attending to the second crowd of guests, who were celebrating a rural wedding in her house. It was busy work to Martha Thomas, yet her smile never flagged; and when Owen Griffiths had finished his evening meal she was there, ready with a hope that it had done him good, and was to his mind, and a word of intelligence that the wedding-folk were about to dance in the kitchen, and the harper was the famous Edward of Corwen.

Owen, partly from good-natured compliance with his hostess's implied wish, and partly from curiosity, lounged to the passage which led to the kitchen—not the every-day, working, cooking kitchen, which was behind, but a good-sized room, where the mistress sat, when her work was done, and where the country people were commonly entertained at such merry-makings as the present. The lintels of the door formed a frame for the animated picture which Owen saw within, as he leaned against the wall in the dark passage. The red light of the fire, with every now and then a falling piece of turf sending forth a fresh blaze, shone full upon four young men who were dancing a measure something like a Scotch reel, keeping admirable time in their rapid movements to the capital tune the harper was playing. They had their hats on when Owen first took his stand, but as they grew more and more animated they flung them away, and presently their shoes were kicked off with like disregard to the spot where they might happen to alight. Shouts of applause followed any remarkable exertion of agility, in which each seemed to try to excel his companions. At length, wearied and exhausted, they sat down, and the harper gradually changed to one of those wild, inspiring national airs for which he was so famous. The thronged audience sat earnest and breathless, and you might have heard a pin drop, except when some maiden passed hurriedly, with flaring candle and busy look, through to the real kitchen beyond. When he had finished his beautiful theme on "The March of the men of Harlech," he changed the measure again to "Tri chant o' bunnan" (Three hundred pounds), and immediately a most unmusical-looking man began chanting "Pennillion," or a sort of recitative stanzas, which were soon taken up by another, and this amusement lasted so long that Owen grew weary, and was thinking of retreating from his post by the door, when some little bustle was occasioned, on the opposite side of the room, by the entrance of a middle-aged man, and a young girl, apparently his daughter. The man advanced to the bench occupied by the seniors of the party, who welcomed him with the usual pretty Welsh greeting, "Pa sut mae dy galon?" ("How is thy heart?") and drinking his health passed on to him the cup of excellent cwrw. The girl, evidently a village belle, was as warmly greeted by the young men, while the girls eyed her rather askance with a half-jealous look, which Owen set down to the score of her extreme prettiness. Like most Welsh women, she was of middle size as to height, but beautifully made, with the most perfect yet delicate roundness in every limb. Her little mob-cap was carefully adjusted to a face which was excessively pretty, though it never could be called handsome. It also was round, with the slightest tendency to the oval shape, richly coloured, though somewhat olive in complexion, with dimples in cheek and chin, and the most scarlet lips Owen had ever seen, that were too short to meet over the small pearly teeth. The nose was the most defective feature; but the eyes were splendid. They were so long, so lustrous, yet at times so very soft under their thick fringe of eyelash! The nut-brown hair was carefully braided beneath the border of delicate lace: it was evident the little village beauty knew how to make the most of all her attractions, for the gay colours which were displayed in her neckerchief were in complete harmony with the complexion.

Owen was much attracted, while yet he was amused, by the evident coquetry the girl displayed, collecting around her a whole bevy of young fellows, for each of whom she seemed to have some gay speech, some attractive look or action. In a few minutes young Griffiths of Bodowen was at her side, brought thither by a variety of idle motives, and as her undivided attention was given to the Welsh heir, her admirers, one by one, dropped off, to seat themselves by some less fascinating but more attentive fair one. The more Owen conversed with the girl, the more he was taken; she had more wit and talent than he had fancied possible; a self-abandon and thoughtfulness, to boot, that seemed full of charms; and then her voice was so clear and sweet, and her actions so full of grace, that Owen was fascinated before he was well aware, and kept looking into her bright, blushing face, till her uplifted flashing eye fell beneath his earnest gaze.

While it thus happened that they were silent—she from confusion at the unexpected warmth of his admiration, he from an unconsciousness of anything but the beautiful changes in her flexile countenance—the man whom Owen took for her father came up and addressed some observation to his daughter, from whence he glided into some commonplace though respectful remark to Owen, and at length engaging him in some slight, local conversation, he led the way to the account of a spot on the peninsula of Penthryn, where teal abounded, and concluded with begging Owen to allow him to show him the exact place, saying that whenever the young Squire felt so inclined, if he would honour him by a call at his house, he would take him across in his boat. While Owen listened, his attention was not so much absorbed as to be unaware that the little beauty at his side was refusing one or two who endeavoured to draw her from her place by invitations to dance. Flattered by his own construction of her refusals, he again directed all his attention to her, till she was called away by her father, who was leaving the scene of festivity. Before he left he reminded Owen of his promise, and added—

"Perhaps, sir, you do not know me. My name is Ellis Pritchard, and I live at Ty Glas, on this side of Moel Gêst; anyone can point it out to you."

When the father and daughter had left, Owen slowly prepared for his ride home; but encountering the hostess, he could not resist asking a few questions relative to Ellis Pritchard and his pretty daughter. She answered shortly but respectfully, and then said, rather hesitatingly —

"Master Griffiths, you know the triad, 'Tri pheth tebyg y naill i'r llall, ysgnbwr heb yd, mail deg heb ddiawd, a merch deg heb ei geirda' (Three things are alike: a fine barn without corn, a fine cup without drink, a fine woman without her reputation)." She hastily quitted him, and Owen rode slowly to his unhappy home.

Ellis Pritchard, half farmer and half fisherman, was shrewd, and keen, and worldly; yet he was good-natured, and sufficiently generous to have become rather a popular man among his equals. He had been struck with the young Squire's attention to his pretty daughter, and was not insensible to the advantages to be derived from it. Nest would not be the first peasant girl, by any means, who had been transplanted to a Welsh manor-house as its mistress; and, accordingly, her father had shrewdly given the admiring young man some pretext for further opportunities of seeing her.

As for Nest herself, she had somewhat of her father's worldliness, and was fully alive to the superior station of her new admirer, and quite prepared to slight all her old sweethearts on his account. But then she had something more of feeling in her reckoning; she had not been insensible to the earnest yet comparatively refined homage which Owen paid her; she had noticed his expressive and occasionally handsome countenance

96

with admiration, and was flattered by his so immediately singling her out from her companions. As to the hint which Martha Thomas had thrown out, it is enough to say that Nest was very giddy, and that she was motherless. She had high spirits and a great love of admiration, or, to use a softer term, she loved to please; men, women, and children, all, she delighted to gladden with her smile and voice. She coquetted, and flirted, and went to the extreme lengths of Welsh courtship, till the seniors of the village shook their heads, and cautioned their daughters against her acquaintance. If not absolutely guilty, she had too frequently been on the verge of guilt.

Even at the time, Martha Thomas's hint made but little impression on Owen, for his senses were otherwise occupied; but in a few days the recollection thereof had wholly died away, and one warm glorious summer's day, he bent his steps toward Ellis Pritchard's with a beating heart; for, except some very slight flirtations at Oxford, Owen had never been touched; his thoughts, his fancy, had been otherwise engaged.

Ty Glas was built against one of the lower rocks of Moel Gêst, which, indeed, formed a side to the low, lengthy house. The materials of the cottage were the shingly stones which had fallen from above, plastered rudely together, with deep recesses for the small oblong windows. Altogether, the exterior was much ruder than Owen had expected; but inside there seemed no lack of comforts. The house was divided into two apartments, one large, roomy, and dark, into which Owen entered immediately; and before the blushing Nest came from the inner chamber (for she had seen the young Squire coming, and hastily gone to make some alteration in her dress), he had had time to look around him, and note the various little particulars of the room. Beneath the window (which commanded a magnificent view) was an oaken dresser, replete with drawers and cupboards, and brightly polished to a rich dark colour. In the farther part of the room Owen could at first distinguish little, entering as he did from the glaring sunlight, but he soon saw that there were two oaken beds, closed up after the manner of the Welsh: in fact, the domitories of Ellis Pritchard and the man who served under him, both on sea and on land. There was the large wheel used for spinning wool, left standing on the middle of the floor, as if in use only a few minutes before; and around the ample chimney hung flitches of bacon, dried kids'-flesh, and fish, that was in process of smoking for winter's store.

Before Nest had shyly dared to enter, her father, who had been mending his nets down below, and seen Owen winding up to the house, came in and gave him a hearty yet respectful welcome; and then Nest, downcast and blushing, full of the consciousness which her father's advice and conversation had not failed to inspire, ventured to join them. To Owen's mind this reserve and shyness gave her new charms.

It was too bright, too hot, too anything to think of going to shoot teal till later in the day, and Owen was delighted to accept a hesitating invitation to share the noonday meal. Some ewe-milk cheese, very hard and dry, oat-cake, slips of the dried kids'-flesh broiled, after having been previously soaked in water for a few minutes, delicious butter and fresh butter-milk, with a liquor called "diod griafol" (made from the berries of the Sorbus aucuparia, infused in water and then fermented), composed the frugal repast; but there was something so clean and neat, and withal such a true welcome, that Owen had seldom enjoyed a meal so much. Indeed, at that time of day the Welsh squires differed from the farmers more in the plenty and rough abundance of their manner of living than in the refinement of style of their table.

At the present day, down in Llyn, the Welsh gentry are not a wit behind their Saxon equals in the expensive elegances of life; but then (when there was but one pewter-service in all Northumberland) there was nothing in Ellis Pritchard's mode of living that grated on the young Squire's sense of refinement.

Little was said by that young pair of wooers during the meal; the father had all the conversation to himself, apparently heedless of the ardent looks and inattentive mien of his guest. As Owen became more serious in his feelings, he grew more timid in their expression, and at night, when they returned from their shooting-excursion, the caress he gave Nest was almost as bashfully offered as received.

This was but the first of a series of days devoted to Nest in reality, though at first he thought some little disguise of his object was necessary. The past, the future, was all forgotten in those happy days of love.

And every worldly plan, every womanly wile was put in practice by Ellis Pritchard and his daughter, to render his visits agreeable and alluring. Indeed, the very circumstance of his being welcome was enough to attract the poor young man, to whom the feeling so produced was new and full of charms. He left a home where the certainty of being thwarted made him chary in expressing his wishes; where no tones of love ever fell

99

on his ear, save those addressed to others; where his presence or absence was a matter of utter indifference; and when he entered Ty Glas, all, down to the little cur which, with clamorous barkings, claimed a part of his attention, seemed to rejoice. His account of his day's employment found a willing listener in Ellis; and when he passed on to Nest, busy at her wheel or at her churn, the deepened colour, the conscious eye, and the gradual yielding of herself up to his lover-like caress, had worlds of charms. Ellis Pritchard was a tenant on the Bodowen estate, and therefore had reasons in plenty for wishing to keep the young Squire's visits secret; and Owen, unwilling to disturb the sunny calm of these halcyon days by any storm at home, was ready to use all the artifice which Ellis suggested as to the mode of his calls at Ty Glas. Nor was he unaware of the probable, nay, the hoped-for termination of these repeated days of happiness. He was quite conscious that the father wished for nothing better than the marriage of his daughter to the heir of Bodowen; and when Nest had hidden her face in his neck, which was encircled by her clasping arms, and murmured into his ear her acknowledgment of love, he felt only too desirous of finding some one to love him for ever. Though not highly principled, he would not have tried to obtain Nest on other terms save those of marriage: he did so pine after enduring love, and fancied he should have bound her heart for evermore to his, when they had taken the solemn oaths of matrimony.

There was no great difficulty attending a secret marriage at such a place and at such a time. One gusty autumn day, Ellis ferried them round Penthryn to Llandutrwyn, and there saw his little Nest become future Lady of Bodowen.

How often do we see giddy, coquetting, restless girls become sobered by marriage? A great object in life is decided; one on which their thoughts have been running in all their vagaries, and they seem to verify the beautiful fable of Undine. A new soul beams out in the gentleness and repose of their future lives. An indescribable softness and tenderness takes place of the wearying vanity of their former endeavours to attract admiration. Something of this sort took place in Nest Pritchard. If at first she had been anxious to attract the young Squire of Bodowen, long before her marriage this feeling had merged into a truer love than she had ever felt before; and now that he was her own, her husband, her whole soul was bent toward making him amends, as far as in her lay, for the misery which, with a woman's tact, she saw that he had to endure at his home. Her greetings were abounding in delicately-expressed love; her study of his tastes unwearying, in the arrangement of her dress, her time, her very thoughts.

No wonder that he looked back on his wedding-day with a thankfulness which is seldom the result of unequal marriages. No wonder that his heart beat aloud as formerly when he wound up the little path to Ty Glas, and saw—keen though the winter's wind might be—that Nest was standing out at the door to watch for his dimly-seen approach, while the candle flared in the little window as a beacon to guide him aright.

The angry words and unkind actions of home fell deadened on his heart; he thought of the love that was surely his, and of the new promise of love that a short time would bring forth, and he could almost have smiled at the impotent efforts to disturb his peace.

A few more months, and the young father was greeted by a feeble little cry, when he hastily entered Ty Glas, one morning early, in consequence of a summons conveyed mysteriously to Bodowen; and the pale mother, smiling, and feebly holding up her babe to its father's kiss, seemed to him even more lovely than the bright gay Nest who had won his heart at the little inn of Penmorfa.

But the curse was at work! The fulfilment of the prophecy was nigh at hand!

CHAPTER II

It was the autumn after the birth of their boy; it had been a glorious summer, with bright, hot, sunny weather; and now the year was fading away as seasonably into mellow days, with mornings of silver mists and clear frosty nights. The blooming look of the time of flowers, was past and gone; but instead there were even richer tints abroad in the sun-coloured leaves, the lichens, the golden blossomed furze; if it was the time of fading, there was a glory in the decay.

Nest, in her loving anxiety to surround her dwelling with every charm for her husband's sake, had turned gardener, and the little corners of the rude court before the house were filled with many a delicate mountain-flower, transplanted more for its beauty than its rarity. The sweetbrier bush may even yet be seen, old and gray, which she and Owen planted a green slipling beneath the window of her little chamber. In those moments Owen forgot all besides the present; all the cares and griefs he had known in the past, and all that might await him of woe and death in the future. The boy, too, was as lovely a child as the fondest parent was ever blessed with; and crowed with delight, and clapped his little hands, as his mother held him in her arms at the cottage-door to watch his father's ascent up the rough path that led to Ty Glas, one bright autumnal morning; and when the three entered the house together, it was difficult to say which was the happiest. Owen carried his boy, and tossed and played with him, while Nest sought out some little article of work, and seated herself on the dresser beneath the window, where now busily plying the needle, and then again looking at her husband, she eagerly told him the little pieces of domestic intelligence, the winning ways of the child, the result of yesterday's fishing, and such of the gossip of Penmorfa as came to the ears of the now retired Nest. She noticed that, when she mentioned any little circumstance which bore the slightest reference to Bodowen, her husband appeared chafed and uneasy, and at last avoided anything that might in the least remind him of home. In truth, he had been suffering much of late from the irritability of his father, shown in trifles to be sure, but not the less galling on that account.

While they were thus talking, and caressing each other and the child, a shadow darkened the room, and before they could catch a glimpse of the object that had occasioned it, it vanished, and Squire Griffiths lifted the door-latch and stood before them. He stood and looked—first on his son, so different, in his buoyant expression of content and enjoyment, with his noble child in his arms, like a proud and happy father, as he was, from the depressed, moody young man he too often appeared at Bodowen; then on Nest—poor, trembling, sickened Nest!—who dropped her work, but yet durst not stir from her seat, on the dresser, while she looked to her husband as if for protection from his father.

The Squire was silent, as he glared from one to the other, his features white with restrained passion. When he spoke, his words came most distinct in their forced composure. It was to his son he addressed himself:

104

"That woman! who is she?"

Owen hesitated one moment, and then replied, in a steady, yet quiet voice:

"Father, that woman is my wife."

He would have added some apology for the long concealment of his marriage; have appealed to his father's forgiveness; but the foam flew from Squire Owen's lips as he burst forth with invective against Nest:—

"You have married her! It is as they told me! Married Nest Pritchard yr buten! And you stand there as if you had not disgraced yourself for ever and ever with your accursed wiving! And the fair harlot sits there, in her mocking modesty, practising the mimming airs that will become her state as future Lady of Bodowen. But I will move heaven and earth before that false woman darken the doors of my father's house as mistress!"

All this was said with such rapidity that Owen had no time for the words that thronged to his lips. "Father!" (he burst forth at length) "Father, whosoever told you that Nest Pritchard was a harlot told you a lie as false as hell! Ay! a lie as false as hell!" he added, in a voice of thunder, while he advanced a step or two nearer to the Squire. And then, in a lower tone, he said—

"She is as pure as your own wife; nay, God help me! as the dear, precious mother who brought me forth, and then left me—with no refuge in a mother's heart—to struggle on through life alone. I tell you Nest is as pure as that dear, dead mother!"

"Fool—poor fool!"

At this moment the child—the little Owen—who had kept gazing from one angry countenance to the other, and with earnest look, trying to understand what had brought the fierce glare into the face where till now he had read nothing but love, in some way attracted the Squire's attention, and increased his wrath.

"Yes," he continued, "poor, weak fool that you are, hugging the child of another as if it were your own offspring!" Owen involuntarily caressed the affrighted child, and half smiled at the implication of his father's words. This the Squire perceived, and raising his voice to a scream of rage, he went on:

"I bid you, if you call yourself my son, to cast away that miserable, shameless woman's offspring; cast it away this instant—this instant!"

In this ungovernable rage, seeing that Owen was far from complying with his command, he snatched the poor infant from the loving arms that held it, and throwing it to his mother, left the house inarticulate with fury.

Nest—who had been pale and still as marble during this terrible dialogue, looking on and listening as if fascinated by the words that smote her heart—opened her arms to receive and cherish her precious babe; but the boy was not destined to reach the white refuge of her breast. The furious action of the Squire had been almost without aim, and the infant fell against the sharp edge of the dresser down on to the stone floor.

Owen sprang up to take the child, but he lay so still, so motionless, that the awe of death came over the father, and he stooped down to gaze more closely. At that moment, the upturned, filmy eyes rolled convulsively—a spasm passed along the body—and the lips, yet warm with kissing, quivered into everlasting rest.

A word from her husband told Nest all. She slid down from her seat, and lay by her little son as corpse-like as he, unheeding all the agonizing endearments and passionate adjurations of her husband. And that poor, desolate husband and father! Scarce one little quarter of an hour, and he had been so blessed in his consciousness of love! the bright promise of many years on his infant's face, and the new, fresh soul beaming forth in its awakened intelligence. And there it was; the little clay image, that would never more gladden up at the sight of him, nor stretch forth to meet his embrace; whose inarticulate, yet most eloquent cooings might haunt him in his dreams, but would never more be heard in waking life again! And by the dead babe, almost as utterly insensate, the poor mother had fallen in a merciful faint—the slandered, heart-pierced Nest! Owen struggled against the sickness that came over him, and busied himself in vain attempts at her restoration.

It was now near noon-day, and Ellis Pritchard came home, little dreaming of the sight that awaited him; but though stunned, he was able to take more effectual measures for his poor daughter's recovery than Owen had done.

By-and-by she showed symptoms of returning sense, and was placed in her own little bed in a darkened room, where, without ever waking to complete consciousness, she fell asleep. Then it was that her husband, suffocated by pressure of miserable thought, gently drew his hand from her tightened clasp, and printing one long soft kiss on her white waxen forehead, hastily stole out of the room, and out of the house.

Near the base of Moel Gêst—it might be a quarter of a mile from Ty Glas—was a little neglected solitary copse, wild and tangled with the trailing branches of the dog-rose and the tendrils of the white bryony. Toward the middle of this thicket a deep crystal pool—a clear mirror for the blue heavens above—and round the margin floated the broad green leaves of the water-lily, and when the regal sun shone down in his noonday glory the flowers arose from their cool depths to welcome and greet him. The copse was musical with many sounds; the warbling of birds rejoicing in its shades, the ceaseless hum of the insects that hovered over the pool, the chime of the distant waterfall, the occasional bleating of the sheep from the mountaintop, were all blended into the delicious harmony of nature.

It had been one of Owen's favourite resorts when he had been a lonely wanderer—a pilgrim in search of love in the years gone by. And thither he went, as if by instinct, when he left Ty Glas; quelling the uprising agony till he should reach that little solitary spot.

It was the time of day when a change in the aspect of the weather so frequently takes place; and the little pool was no longer the reflection of a blue and sunny sky: it sent back the dark and slaty clouds above, and, every now and then, a rough gust shook the painted autumn leaves from their branches, and all other music was lost in the sound of the wild winds piping down from the moorlands, which lay up and beyond the clefts in the mountain-side. Presently the rain came on and beat down in torrents.

But Owen heeded it not. He sat on the dank ground, his face buried in his hands, and his whole strength, physical and mental, employed in quelling the rush of blood, which rose and boiled and gurgled in his brain as if it would madden him.

The phantom of his dead child rose ever before him, and seemed to cry aloud for vengeance. And when the poor young man thought upon the victim whom he required in his wild longing for revenge, he shuddered, for it was his father!

Again and again he tried not to think; but still the circle of thought came round, eddying through his brain. At length he mastered his passions, and they were calm; then he forced himself to arrange some plan for the future.

He had not, in the passionate hurry of the moment, seen that his father had left the cottage before he was aware of the fatal accident that befell the child. Owen thought he had seen all; and once he planned to go to the Squire and tell him of the anguish of heart he had wrought, and awe him, as it were, by the dignity of grief. But then again he durst not—he distrusted his self-control—the old prophecy rose up in its horror—he dreaded his doom.

At last he determined to leave his father for ever; to take Nest to some distant country where she might forget her firstborn, and where he himself might gain a livelihood by his own exertions.

But when he tried to descend to the various little arrangements which were involved in the execution of this plan, he remembered that all his money (and in this respect Squire Griffiths was no niggard) was locked up in his escritoire at Bodowen. In vain he tried to do away with this matter-of-fact difficulty; go to Bodowen he must: and his only hope—nay his determination—was to avoid his father.

He rose and took a by-path to Bodowen. The house looked even more gloomy and desolate than usual in the heavy down-pouring rain, yet Owen gazed on it with something of regret—for sorrowful as his days in it had been, he was about to leave it for many many years, if not for ever. He entered by a side door opening into a passage that led to his own room, where he kept his books, his guns, his fishing-tackle, his writing materials, et cetera.

Here he hurriedly began to select the few articles he intended to take; for, besides the dread of interruption, he was feverishly anxious to travel far that very night, if only Nest was capable of performing the journey. As he was thus employed, he tried to conjecture what his father's feelings would be on finding that his once-loved son was gone away for ever. Would he then awaken to regret for the conduct which had driven him from home, and bitterly think on the loving and caressing boy who haunted his footsteps in former days? Or, alas! would he only feel that an obstacle to his daily happiness—to his contentment with his wife, and his strange, doting affection for the child—was taken away? Would they make merry over the heir's departure? Then he thought of Nest—the young childless mother, whose heart had not yet realized her fulness of desolation. Poor Nest! so loving as she was, so devoted to her child—how should he console her? He pictured her away in a strange land, pining for her native mountains, and refusing to be comforted because her child was not.

Even this thought of the home-sickness that might possibly beset Nest hardly made him hesitate in his determination; so strongly had the idea taken possession of him that only by putting miles and leagues between him and his father could he avert the doom which seemed blending itself with the very purposes of his life as long as he stayed in proximity with the slayer of his child.

He had now nearly completed his hasty work of preparation, and was full of tender thoughts of his wife, when the door opened, and the elfish Robert peered in, in search of some of his brother's possessions. On seeing Owen he hesitated, but then came boldly forward, and laid his hand on Owen's arm, saying,

"Nesta yr buten! How is Nest yr buten?"

He looked maliciously into Owen's face to mark the effect of his words, but was terrified at the expression he read there. He started off and ran to the door, while Owen tried to check himself, saying continually, "He is but a child. He does not understand the meaning of what he says. He is but a child!" Still Robert, now in fancied security, kept calling out his insulting words, and Owen's hand was on his gun, grasping it as if to restrain his rising fury.

But when Robert passed on daringly to mocking words relating to the poor dead child, Owen could bear it no longer; and before the boy was well aware, Owen was fiercely holding him in an iron clasp with one hand, while he struck him hard with the other.

In a minute he checked himself. He paused, relaxed his grasp, and, to his horror, he saw Robert sink to the ground; in fact, the lad was half-stunned, half-frightened, and thought it best to assume insensibility.

Owen—miserable Owen—seeing him lie there prostrate, was bitterly repentant, and would have dragged him to the carved settle, and done all he could to restore him to his senses, but at this instant the Squire came in.

Probably, when the household at Bodowen rose that morning, there was but one among them ignorant of the heir's relation to Nest Pritchard and her child; for secret as he tried to make his visits to Ty Glas, they had been too frequent not to be noticed, and Nest's altered conduct—no longer frequenting dances and merry-makings—was a strongly corroborative circumstance. But Mrs. Griffiths' influence reigned paramount, if unacknowledged, at Bodowen, and till she sanctioned the disclosure, none would dare to tell the Squire.

Now, however, the time drew near when it suited her to make her husband aware of the connection his son had formed; so, with many tears, and much seeming reluctance, she broke the intelligence to him—taking good care, at the same time, to inform him of the light character Nest had borne. Nor did she confine this evil reputation to her conduct before her marriage, but insinuated that even to this day she was a "woman of the grove and brake"—for centuries the Welsh term of opprobrium for the loosest female characters.

Squire Griffiths easily tracked Owen to Ty Glas; and without any aim but the gratification of his furious anger, followed him to upbraid as we have seen. But he left the cottage even more enraged against his son than he had entered it, and returned home to hear the evil suggestions of the stepmother. He had heard a slight scuffle in which he caught the tones of Robert's voice, as he passed along the hall, and an instant afterwards he saw the apparently lifeless body of his little favourite dragged along by the culprit Owen—the marks of strong passion yet visible on his face. Not loud, but bitter and deep were the evil words which the father bestowed on the son; and as Owen stood proudly and sullenly silent, disdaining all exculpation of himself in the presence of one who had wrought him so much graver— so fatal an injury—Robert's mother entered the room. At sight of her natural emotion the wrath of the Squire was redoubled, and his wild suspicions that this violence of Owen's to Robert was a premeditated act appeared like the proven truth through the mists of rage. He summoned domestics as if to guard his own and his wife's life from the attempts of his son; and the servants stood wondering around—now gazing at Mrs. Griffiths, alternately scolding and sobbing, while she tried to restore the lad from his really bruised and half-unconscious state; now at the fierce and angry Squire; and now at the sad and silent Owen. And he—he was hardly aware of their looks of wonder and terror; his father's words fell on a deadened ear; for before his eyes there rose a pale dead babe, and in that lady's violent sounds of grief he heard the wailing of a more sad, more hopeless mother. For by this time the lad Robert had opened his eyes, and though evidently suffering a good deal from the effects of Owen's blows, was fully conscious of all that was passing around him.

Had Owen been left to his own nature, his heart would have worked itself to doubly love the boy whom he had injured; but he was stubborn from injustice, and hardened by suffering. He refused to vindicate himself; he made no effort to resist the imprisonment the Squire had decreed, until a surgeon's opinion of the real extent of Robert's injuries was made known. It was not until the door was locked and barred, as if upon some wild and furious beast, that the recollection of poor Nest, without his comforting presence, came into his mind. Oh! thought he, how she would be wearying, pining for his tender sympathy; if, indeed, she had recovered the shock of mind sufficiently to be sensible of consolation! What would she think of his absence? Could she imagine he believed his father's words, and had left her, in this her sore trouble and bereavement? The thought madened him, and he looked around for some mode of escape.

He had been confined in a small unfurnished room on the first floor, wainscoted, and carved all round, with a massy door, calculated to resist the attempts of a dozen strong men, even had he afterward been able to escape from the house unseen, unheard. The window was placed (as is common in old Welsh houses) over the fire-place; with branching chimneys on either hand, forming a sort of projection on the outside. By this outlet his escape was easy, even had he been less determined and desperate than he was. And when he had descended, with a little care, a little winding, he might elude all observation and pursue his original intention of going to Ty Glas.

The storm had abated, and watery sunbeams were gilding the bay, as Owen descended from the window, and, stealing along in the broad afternoon shadows, made his way to the little plateau of green turf in the garden at the top of a steep precipitous rock, down the abrupt face of which he had often dropped, by means of a well-secured rope, into the small sailing-boat (his father's present, alas! in days gone by) which lay moored in the deep sea-water below. He had always kept his boat there, because it was the nearest available spot to the house; but before he could reach the place—unless, indeed, he crossed a broad sun-lighted piece of ground in full view of the windows on that side of the house, and without the shadow of a single sheltering tree or shrub—he had to skirt round a rude semicircle of underwood, which would have been considered as a shrubbery had any one taken pains with it. Step by step he stealthily moved along—hearing voices now, again seeing his father and stepmother in no distant walk, the Squire evidently caressing and consoling his wife, who seemed to be urging some point with great vehemence, again forced to crouch down to avoid being seen by the cook, returning from the rude kitchen-garden with a handful of herbs. This was the way the doomed heir of Bodowen left his ancestral house for ever, and hoped to leave behind him his doom. At length he reached the plateau— he breathed more freely. He stooped to discover the hidden coil of rope, kept safe and dry in a hole under a great round flat piece of rock: his head was bent down; he did not see his father approach, nor did he hear his footstep for the rush of blood to his head in the stooping effort of lifting the stone; the Squire had grappled with him before he rose up again, before he fully knew whose hands detained him, now, when his liberty of person and action seemed secure. He made a vigorous struggle to free himself; he wrestled with his father for a moment—he pushed him hard, and drove him on to the great displaced stone, all unsteady in its balance.

115

Down went the Squire, down into the deep waters below—down after him went Owen, half consciously, half unconsciously, partly compelled by the sudden cessation of any opposing body, partly from a vehement irrepressible impulse to rescue his father. But he had instinctively chosen a safer place in the deep seawater pool than that into which his push had sent his father. The Squire had hit his head with much violence against the side of the boat, in his fall; it is, indeed, doubtful whether he was not killed before ever he sank into the sea. But Owen knew nothing save that the awful doom seemed even now present. He plunged down, he dived below the water in search of the body which had none of the elasticity of life to buoy it up; he saw his father in those depths, he clutched at him, he brought him up and cast him, a dead weight, into the boat, and exhausted by the effort, he had begun himself to sink again before he instinctively strove to rise and climb into the rocking boat. There lay his father, with a deep dent in the side of his head where the skull had been fractured by his fall; his face blackened by the arrested course of the blood. Owen felt his pulse, his heart—all was still. He called him by his name.

"Father, father!" he cried, "come back! come back! You never knew how I loved you! how I could love you still—if—Oh God!"

And the thought of his little child rose before him. "Yes, father," he cried afresh, "you never knew how he fell—how he died! Oh, if I had but had patience to tell you! If you would but have borne with me and listened! And now it is over! Oh father! father!"

Whether she had heard this wild wailing voice, or whether it

116

was only that she missed her husband and wanted him for some little every-day question, or, as was perhaps more likely, she had discovered Owen's escape, and come to inform her husband of it, I do not know, but on the rock, right above his head, as it seemed, Owen heard his stepmother calling her husband.

He was silent, and softly pushed the boat right under the rock till the sides grated against the stones, and the overhanging branches concealed him and it from all not on a level with the water. Wet as he was, he lay down by his dead father the better to conceal himself; and, somehow, the action recalled those early days of childhood—the first in the Squire's widowhood—when Owen had shared his father's bed, and used to waken him in the morning to hear one of the old Welsh legends. How long he lay thus—body chilled, and brain hard-working through the heavy pressure of a reality as terrible as a nightmare—he never knew; but at length he roused himself up to think of Nest.

Drawing out a great sail, he covered up the body of his father with it where he lay in the bottom of the boat. Then with his numbed hands he took the oars, and pulled out into the more open sea toward Criccaeth. He skirted along the coast till he found a shadowed cleft in the dark rocks; to that point he rowed, and anchored his boat close in land. Then he mounted, staggering, half longing to fall into the dark waters and be at rest—half instinctively finding out the surest foot-rests on that precipitous face of rock, till he was high up, safe landed on the turfy summit. He ran off, as if pursued, toward Penmorfa; he ran with maddened energy. Suddenly he paused, turned, ran again with the same speed, and threw himself prone on the summit, looking down into his boat with straining eyes to see if

117

there had been any movement of life—any displacement of a fold of sail-cloth. It was all quiet deep down below, but as he gazed the shifting light gave the appearance of a slight movement. Owen ran to a lower part of the rock, stripped, plunged into the water, and swam to the boat. When there, all was still—awfully still! For a minute or two, he dared not lift up the cloth. Then reflecting that the same terror might beset him again—of leaving his father unaided while yet a spark of life lingered—he removed the shrouding cover. The eyes looked into his with a dead stare! He closed the lids and bound up the jaw. Again he looked. This time he raised himself out of the water and kissed the brow.

"It was my doom, father! It would have been better if I had died at my birth!"

Daylight was fading away. Precious daylight! He swam back, dressed, and set off afresh for Penmorfa. When he opened the door of Ty Glas, Ellis Pritchard looked at him reproachfully, from his seat in the darkly-shadowed chimney-corner.

"You're come at last," said he. "One of our kind (i.e., station) would not have left his wife to mourn by herself over her dead child; nor would one of our kind have let his father kill his own true son. I've a good mind to take her from you for ever."

"I did not tell him," cried Nest, looking piteously at her husband; "he made me tell him part, and guessed the rest."

She was nursing her babe on her knee as if it was alive. Owen stood before Ellis Pritchard.

"Be silent," said he, quietly. "Neither words nor deeds but what are decreed can come to pass. I was set to do my work, this hundred years and more. The time waited for me, and the man waited for me. I have done what was foretold of me for generations!"

Ellis Pritchard knew the old tale of the prophecy, and believed in it in a dull, dead kind of way, but somehow never thought it would come to pass in his time. Now, however, he understood it all in a moment, though he mistook Owen's nature so much as to believe that the deed was intentionally done, out of revenge for the death of his boy; and viewing it in this light, Ellis thought it little more than a just punishment for the cause of all the wild despairing sorrow he had seen his only child suffer during the hours of this long afternoon. But he knew the law would not so regard it. Even the lax Welsh law of those days could not fail to examine into the death of a man of Squire Griffith's standing. So the acute Ellis thought how he could conceal the culprit for a time.

"Come," said he; "don't look so scared! It was your doom, not your fault;" and he laid a hand on Owen's shoulder.

"You're wet," said he, suddenly. "Where have you been? Nest, your husband is dripping, drookit wet. That's what makes him look so blue and wan."

Nest softly laid her baby in its cradle; she was half stupefied with crying, and had not understood to what Owen alluded, when he spoke of his doom being fulfilled, if indeed she had heard the words.

Her touch thawed Owen's miserable heart.

"Oh, Nest!" said he, clasping her in his arms; "do you love me still—can you love me, my own darling?"

"Why not?" asked she, her eyes filling with tears. "I only love you more than ever, for you were my poor baby's father!"

"But, Nest—Oh, tell her, Ellis! you know."

"No need, no need!" said Ellis. "She's had enough to think on. Bustle, my girl, and get out my Sunday clothes."

"I don't understand," said Nest, putting her hand up to her head. "What is to tell? and why are you so wet? God help me for a poor crazed thing, for I cannot guess at the meaning of your words and your strange looks! I only know my baby is dead!" and she burst into tears.

"Come, Nest! go and fetch him a change, quick!" and as she meekly obeyed, too languid to strive further to understand, Ellis said rapidly to Owen, in a low, hurried voice—

"Are you meaning that the Squire is dead? Speak low, lest she hear. Well, well, no need to talk about how he died. It was sudden, I see; and we must all of us die; and he'll have to be buried. It's well the night is near. And I should not wonder now if you'd like to travel for a bit; it would do Nest a power of good; and then—there's many a one goes out of his own house and never comes back again; and—I trust he's not lying in his own house—and there's a stir for a bit, and a search, and a wonder—and, by-and-by, the heir just steps in, as quiet as can be. And that's what you'll do, and bring Nest to Bodowen after

120

all. Nay, child, better stockings nor those; find the blue woollens I bought at Llanrwst fair. Only don't lose heart. It's done now and can't be helped. It was the piece of work set you to do from the days of the Tudors, they say. And he deserved it. Look in yon cradle. So tell us where he is, and I'll take heart of grace and see what can be done for him."

But Owen sat wet and haggard, looking into the peat fire as if for visions of the past, and never heeding a word Ellis said. Nor did he move when Nest brought the armful of dry clothes.

"Come, rouse up, man!" said Ellis, growing impatient. But he neither spoke nor moved.

"What is the matter, father?" asked Nest, bewildered.

Ellis kept on watching Owen for a minute or two, till on his daughter's repetition of the question, he said—

"Ask him yourself, Nest."

"Oh, husband, what is it?" said she, kneeling down and bringing her face to a level with his.

"Don't you know?" said he, heavily. "You won't love me when you do know. And yet it was not my doing: it was my doom."

"What does he mean, father?" asked Nest, looking up; but she caught a gesture from Ellis urging her to go on questioning her husband.

"I will love you, husband, whatever has happened. Only let me know the worst."

121

A pause, during which Nest and Ellis hung breathless.

"My father is dead, Nest."

Nest caught her breath with a sharp gasp.

"God forgive him!" said she, thinking on her babe.

"God forgive me!" said Owen.

"You did not—" Nest stopped.

"Yes, I did. Now you know it. It was my doom. How could I help it? The devil helped me—he placed the stone so that my father fell. I jumped into the water to save him. I did, indeed, Nest. I was nearly drowned myself. But he was dead—dead—killed by the fall!"

"Then he is safe at the bottom of the sea?" said Ellis, with hungry eagerness.

"No, he is not; he lies in my boat," said Owen, shivering a little, more at the thought of his last glimpse at his father's face than from cold.

"Oh, husband, change your wet clothes!" pleaded Nest, to whom the death of the old man was simply a horror with which she had nothing to do, while her husband's discomfort was a present trouble.

While she helped him to take off the wet garments which he would never have had energy enough to remove of himself, Ellis was busy preparing food, and mixing a great tumbler of spirits and hot water. He stood over the unfortunate young man and compelled him to eat and drink, and made Nest, too, taste some mouthfuls—all the while planning in his own mind how best to conceal what had been done, and who had done it; not altogether without a certain feeling of vulgar triumph in the reflection that Nest, as she stood there, carelessly dressed, dishevelled in her grief, was in reality the mistress of Bodowen, than which Ellis Pritchard had never seen a grander house, though he believed such might exist.

By dint of a few dexterous questions he found out all he wanted to know from Owen, as he ate and drank. In fact, it was almost a relief to Owen to dilute the horror by talking about it. Before the meal was done, if meal it could be called, Ellis knew all he cared to know.

"Now, Nest, on with your cloak and haps. Pack up what needs to go with you, for both you and your husband must be half way to Liverpool by to-morrow's morn. I'll take you past Rhyl Sands in my fishing-boat, with yours in tow; and, once over the dangerous part, I'll return with my cargo of fish, and learn how much stir there is at Bodowen. Once safe hidden in Liverpool, no one will know where you are, and you may stay quiet till your time comes for returning."

"I will never come home again," said Owen, doggedly. "The place is accursed!"

"Hoot! be guided by me, man. Why, it was but an accident, after all! And we'll land at the Holy Island, at the Point of Llyn; there is an old cousin of mine, the parson, there—for the Pritchards have known better days, Squire—and we'll bury him there. It was but an accident, man. Hold up your head! You and Nest will come home yet and fill Bodowen with children, and I'll live to see it."

"Never!" said Owen. "I am the last male of my race, and the son has murdered his father!"

Nest came in laden and cloaked. Ellis was for hurrying them off. The fire was extinguished, the door was locked.

"Here, Nest, my darling, let me take your bundle while I guide you down the steps." But her husband bent his head, and spoke never a word. Nest gave her father the bundle (already loaded with such things as he himself had seen fit to take), but clasped another softly and tightly.

"No one shall help me with this," said she, in a low voice.

Her father did not understand her; her husband did, and placed his strong helping arm round her waist, and blessed her.

"We will all go together, Nest," said he. "But where?" and he looked up at the storm-tossed clouds coming up from windward.

"It is a dirty night," said Ellis, turning his head round to speak to his companions at last. "But never fear, we'll weather it?" And he made for the place where his vessel was moored. Then he stopped and thought a moment.

"Stay here!" said he, addressing his companions. "I may meet folk, and I shall, maybe, have to hear and to speak. You wait here till I come back for you." So they sat down close together in a corner of the path.

"Let me look at him, Nest!" said Owen.

She took her little dead son out from under her shawl; they looked at his waxen face long and tenderly; kissed it, and covered it up reverently and softly.

"Nest," said Owen, at last, "I feel as though my father's spirit had been near us, and as if it had bent over our poor little one. A strange chilly air met me as I stooped over him. I could fancy the spirit of our pure, blameless child guiding my father's safe over the paths of the sky to the gates of heaven, and escaping those accursed dogs of hell that were darting up from the north in pursuit of souls not five minutes since.

"Don't talk so, Owen," said Nest, curling up to him in the darkness of the copse. "Who knows what may be listening?"

The pair were silent, in a kind of nameless terror, till they heard Ellis Pritchard's loud whisper. "Where are ye? Come along, soft and steady. There were folk about even now, and the Squire is missed, and madam in a fright."

They went swiftly down to the little harbour, and embarked on board Ellis's boat. The sea heaved and rocked even there; the torn clouds went hurrying overhead in a wild tumultuous manner.

They put out into the bay; still in silence, except when some word of command was spoken by Ellis, who took the management of the vessel. They made for the rocky shore, where Owen's boat had been moored. It was not there. It had broken loose and disappeared.

Owen sat down and covered his face. This last event, so simple and natural in itself, struck on his excited and superstitious mind in an extraordinary manner. He had hoped for a certain reconciliation, so to say, by laying his father and his child both in one grave. But now it appeared to him as if there was to be no forgiveness; as if his father revolted even in death against any such peaceful union. Ellis took a practical view of the case. If the Squire's body was found drifting about in a boat known to belong to his son, it would create terrible suspicion as to the manner of his death. At one time in the evening, Ellis had thought of persuading Owen to let him bury the Squire in a sailor's grave; or, in other words, to sew him up in a spare sail, and weighting it well, sink it for ever. He had not broached the subject, from a certain fear of Owen's passionate repugnance to the plan; otherwise, if he had consented, they might have returned to Penmorfa, and passively awaited the course of events, secure of Owen's succession to Bodowen, sooner or later; or if Owen was too much overwhelmed by what had happened, Ellis would have advised him to go away for a short time, and return when the buzz and the talk was over.

Now it was different. It was absolutely necessary that they should leave the country for a time. Through those stormy waters they must plough their way that very night. Ellis had no fear—would have had no fear, at any rate, with Owen as he had been a week, a day ago; but with Owen wild, despairing, helpless, fate-pursued, what could he do?

They sailed into the tossing darkness, and were never more seen of men.

The house of Bodowen has sunk into damp, dark ruins; and a Saxon stranger holds the lands of the Griffiths.

www.ingramcontent.com/pod-product-compliance
Lightning Source LLC
Chambersburg PA
CBHW011515170626
46810CB00009B/3382